OSCAR DANBY, V.C.

A TALE OF THE GREAT EUROPEAN WAR

BY

ROWLAND WALKER

AUTHOR OF " BUCKLE OF SUBMARINE V2," " UNDER WOLFE'S FLAG,'
ETC.

British Library Cataloguing-in-Publication Data
A catalogue record for this book is available from the
British Library

World War One in Literature

In 1939, the writer Robert Graves was asked to write an article for the BBC's *Listener* magazine, explaining 'as a war poet of the last war, why so little poetry has so far been produced by this one.' From the very first weeks of fighting the First World War inspired enormous amounts of poetry, factual analysis, autobiography and fiction - from all countries involved in the conflict. 2,225 English war poets have been counted, of whom 1808 were civilians. The 'total' nature of this war perhaps goes someway to explaining its enormous impact on the popular imagination. Even today, commemorations and the effects of a 'lost generation' are still being witnessed, it was a war fought for traditional, nationalistic values of the nineteenth century, propagated using twentieth century technological and industrial methods of killing. The literature written during, and inspired by the first world war provides extraordinary insight into how the common soldier experienced life in battle, as well as how the civilian population mobilised and dealt with these losses.

A lot of the literature written during the war was designed to inform and propagandise, nowhere more evident than in writing for children. There were many overt attempts to encourage support for the war effort, influencing children's (future soldiers) attitudes towards armed conflict. An earlier example, encouraging children to be good citizens, fighting for king and country was *Scouting for Boys,* written by Lord Baden-Powell, the founder of the scouting movement (published 1908). The cover depicted a boy watching out for enemy ships on the shoreline, replacing traditional images of childish innocence, passivity and naivety with children ready, willing and able to serve their nation. These were activities full of excitement and adventure, including tracking, woodcraft, endurance, chivalry, saving lives and patriotism. Such tropes were eagerly expanded once the war had began, notably by

A.R. Hope, with *The School of Arms: Stories of Boy Soldiers and Sailors* (1915).

This volume contained many stories about the experiences of young soldiers in battles, using historical accounts to make participating in war seen normal. In fact, such actions were often depicted as a fundamental part of any boys coming of age, thereby preparing people to accept the idea of their young men and boys fighting and dying in battle. In the popular children's periodical, *The Boys Own Paper,* numerous stories of young war heroes also provided entertainment for its avid readers - instilling pride in ones own country and distain for the enemy. Despite these glorifying aspects of home-front propaganda, the war literature that is most celebrated today is that which highlights the grim reality and everyday experiences of the men on the front line. From Hemingway's *A Farewell to Arms*, to Remarque's *All Quiet on the Western Front,* to the poetry of Sassoon, Graves, and Brooke, there are numerous examples of acclaimed writing inspired by the Great War. Wilfred Owen (killed in the conflict at the age of twenty-five), wrote in introduction to his collected poems, 'This book is not about heroes... Nor is it about deeds, or lands, nor anything about glory, honour, might, majesty, dominion, or power, except War.... My subject is War, and the pity of War. The Poetry is in the pity.'

The autobiography of Robert Graves perfectly sums up this mood, his 'bitter leave-taking of England.' The title, *Good-Bye to All That* points to the passing of an old order following the cataclysm of global war, the massive inadequacies of the patriotism which the government tried so hard to sustain, the rise of atheism, feminism, socialism and fascism as well as a whole host of other social changes. The unsentimental and frequently comic treatment of the banalities and intensities of the life of a British army officer in the First World War gave the author fame and financial security. It also provided an eager public with detailed descriptions of trench warfare, including the tragic incompetence of the Battle of Loos and the bitter fighting in the first phase of the Somme Offensive. The spread of education in Europe in the decades leading up to World War One meant that both soldiers and the public, at all levels of society, were literate. As a result, authors, both professional and amateur, were prolific during and after the war and found a market for their works. Literature was produced throughout the war but it was in the late 1920s and early 1930s that the real boom in war writing took place.

Erich Maria Remarque's best-selling book, *Im Westen nichts Neues* (*All Quiet on the Western Front*), was translated into 28 languages with world sales nearly reaching 4 million in 1930. The book describes the German soldiers' extreme physical and mental stress during the war, and the detachment from civilian life felt by many of these soldiers upon returning home from the front. Remarque's book was also partly based on Henri Barbusse's 1916 novel, *Le Feu (Under Fire)*. Barbusse was a French journalist who served as a stretcher-bearer on the front lines and his book was very influential in its own right at the time. The year after its publication, it won the prestigious Prix Goncourt and by the Armistice had sold 200,000 copies in France alone. Other novels, such as the *The Good Soldier Švejk* by Jaroslav Hašek, have since become national emblems. This darkly comic tale, and its main protagonist Švejk, has developed into the Czech national personification, exploring both the pointlessness and futility of conflict in general, and of military discipline, Austrian military discipline in particular. Many of its characters, especially the Czechs, were participating in a conflict they did not understand on behalf of a country to which they had no loyalty.

Aside from literature directly relating to combatants experiences, some pre-existing popular literary characters were placed by their authors in World War I-related adventures during or directly after the war. These include Tom Swift (*Tom Swift and His Aerial Warship*, 1915 and *Tom*

Swift and His Air Scout, 1919), Sherlock Holmes (*His Last Bow*, 1917) and Tarzan (*Tarzan the Untamed*, 1920). In addition, there was a massive amount of literature written by those 'left behind' on the home front; Vera Brittain's *Testament of Youth* (first published 1933) has since been acclaimed as a classic for its description of the impact of the war on the lives of women and the civilian population - extending into the post-war years. As is evident, the literature of World War One is an enormous field, encompassing a wide array of styles; propagandistic, poetic, fictional, autobiographical and comical. It provides a glimpse into just what this terrible war meant for the everyday population, as well as the intelligentsia. It is hoped the current reader is encouraged to find out more, and enjoys this book.

This book is part of the World War One Centenary series; creating, collating and reprinting new and old works of poetry, fiction, autobiography and analysis. The series forms a commemorative tribute to mark the passing of one of the world's bloodiest wars, offering new perspectives on this tragic yet fascinating period of human history.

PREFACE

THE GREAT WAR OF 1914 opened the
floodgates of hatred between the nations
which took part and this stirring story,
written when feelings were at their highest,
conveys a true impression of the attitude
adopted towards our enemies. No epithet
was considered too strong for a German,
and whilst the narrative thus portrays
the real atmosphere and conditions under
which the tragic event was fought out it
should be borne in mind that the animosities
engendered by war are now happily a thing
of the past. Therefore, the reader, whilst
enjoying to the full this thrilling tale, will
do well to remember that old enmities have
passed away and that we are now reconciled
to the Central Powers who were opposed
to us.

CONTENTS

CONTENTS

OSCAR DANBY, V.C.

CHAPTER I.

THE SCOUTS' CAMP.

Night sunk upon the dusky beach,
  And in the purple sea;
Such night in England ne'er had been,
  Nor e'er again shall be.

BEHIND a bank of blood-red clouds the sun
had dipped into the sea. His parting shafts
of fire had laid a crimson trail along the deep;
it was but a presage of the coming storm. It
was early in August, 1914, and the war cloud
which had long threatened Europe was ready
to burst. Even now the Kaiser's legions, over-
confident of victory, were marching upon
Belgium. France and Russia were waiting
breathlessly, but England was watching the
gates of the sea.

The Eagle Patrol, a body of first-class
scouts, were spending a week in camp at
Overstrand on the Norfolk coast. They were

mostly fifth form boys from the Old Eliza-
bethan Grammar School at Cockfosters, near
London, and they were enjoying themselves
immensely, for the July exams. were now a
matter of history, and the long vacation was
before them. Willoughby, the youngest, was
fifteen, while Oscar Danby, the patrol-leader,
was just turned sixteen, and the rest were all
somewhere between.

Full of vigour and the restless energy of
youth, the Eagles were at once both the envy
and the admiration of all lesser boys. Many
wonderful stories were current, in the neighbourhood of the school, of their prowess and
skill. Some of these had even reached the
local papers, and the village folk had been
stirred more than once by tales of heroism
and deeds of daring performed by the Eagles.

In the eyes of the school, every member of
the patrol was a hero and a gentleman. His
word was implicitly trusted, and his every
command obeyed with alacrity by every junior.
So far, no one had ever challenged the state-
ment made by John Holland, Esquire, Master
of Arts, Master of English, French, German,
Mathematics, and a great many other things

too numerous to mention—but most sacred of all, SCOUT-MASTER. And what was this challenge that their leader had made? Simply this . . . that the Eagles were the most efficient patrol in England, or, for that matter, in Europe.

But the Eagles were what John Holland had made them, and their worship of him was so great that they were ready at his bidding to do anything, to go anywhere, and to dare everything. And now at last the time was near at hand when their fidelity and courage were about to be put to the severest test, for the wonderful and daring adventures of the Eagle Patrol, as told to the author by one of their number, and the eminent services which they rendered to their country during the great European War, as proved by the honours paid to them by a grateful king and country, seem more like romance than reality.

Thus it happened that on that fatal day, Tuesday, the Fourth of August, 1914, the Eagles clustered about the top of the cliff, where they held their camp, to watch the sun dip into the sea, for, at this point of the coast, at certain times of the year, the sun both rises

and sets in the sea. After sunset came the
dusk, and, as the stars began to twinkle
through the gloom, some of the lads began to
unroll their blankets ready for the night
bivouac, for, after their long day's exercise in
the open air, they were heavy with fatigue.
John Holland, however, still seemed to be
wrapped in deep meditation, gazing across the
sea, as though trying to unravel some great
mystery out yonder, in the gloom of the fading
horizon.

What was the scout-master thinking about?
What could he see out there? Phantom
ships? Those smudgy blurs out there in the
falling dusk, what might they be? Were they
creatures of his own imagination, or were the
enemy destroyers already creeping in?

There was an air of mystery about the
whole camp too, something shadowy and un-
real. It seemed to pervade the whole atmosphere, and infect every member of the patrol
with its spirit. What could it be? What did
it portend? There were no songs in the camp
to-night, no laughter even. Things were not
as usual. The Eagles were now sitting about
the fire, but they spoke in hollow whispers,

and their voices sounded strange and distant. Every now and then they glanced almost furtively at the dark figure of their leader silhouetted against the sky-line.

Suddenly a shower of sparks rose up from the fire and burst into a spurt of flame, as Willoughby, whose *fatigue* it was to tend the camp fire, threw a bundle of dried sticks and twigs upon the half-burnt embers. For a brief moment the whole scene was lighted up, and the ruddy faces of the scouts showed up as though in a picture. An owl, startled from its resting-place in the half-ruined tower, uttered a weird cry, and flew swiftly across the camp.

Then it was that John Holland also started from his reverie, and, recovering himself quickly, cried :—

"Murphy, sound the tattoo! The Eagles will turn in."

"Yes, sir," came the ready response, as the bugler of the patrol sprang to attention, saluted his chief, and then awoke the echoes of land and sea with the solemn notes of the "Last post."

Soon after, "Lights out" was sounded, and the strains of music had scarcely died away, before the Eagles were rolled up snugly in their blankets, seeking that welcome repose which nature gives to those who toil in the open. Long after every scout was fast asleep, however, John Holland still kept his lonely vigil, asking himself a thousand questions without finding an answer.

Out yonder the mast-head lights of a steamer showed where a collier, heavily laden, ploughed its furrow on the deep, making for the Thames, while nearer still, two snake-like forms crept in without lights, then suddenly flashed out a few points on the Morse code, as they spoke to the coast-guard station at Cromer, after which they quickly disappeared again into the now settled gloom.

"That looks like war, at any rate!" murmured the scout-master to himself, as he watched the flashes, and tried to uncode the message but failed.

"What shall I do if this terrible war should come after all? Shall I leave these lads of the Eagle Patrol, and join the regiment to which my younger brother has just been gazetted? If war comes, England will need every son of hers who can carry a rifle! And yet, it will be hard to leave these lads, and tear myself away from them ! " These were some of the thoughts that chased themselves through the mind of John Holland.

As he turned for a moment, he could indistinctly, by the fitful light of the fire, see the sleeping forms of the scouts. Yes, he had trained them, not only in Mathematics and English, but in Scout-craft, until he had made them as efficient as possible. If war came, how he would like to lead these daring, resolute lads to the front! They would be of incalculable assistance to any regiment or brigade to which they might have the good fortune to be attached as auxiliaries. Of that he was quite certain. And yet, even if they offered their services, he felt sure that they would be refused. Thus, for an hour or more, John Holland revolved scheme after scheme in his active brain, until, at length, he too became tired. Then, rolling himself in his rug, he also sought refuge in sleep.

After that, a silence deep and profound fell upon the camp, broken only by the occasional cry of the fern-owl, or the night-jar, as they chased the bats, which wheeled swiftly about the place after still smaller fry, in the shape of insects and moths.

The cloud bank on the horizon gradually melted away, and the constellations silently climbed to the meridian, hanging like rich jewels in the midnight sky. It wanted but a few hours to dawn, when Oscar Danby the patrol-leader opened his eyes, unrolled his blanket, and, half-raising himself from the ground, listened intently to some mysterious yet not unfamiliar sound, which had disturbed his rest.

"What was that?" he asked himself, looking warily around, for his sleep had been full of wild, fantastic and even warlike dreams. Once more the sound reached his ears :—

"Zur-zip-zur, zip-zur-zip, zip-zip !"

Half-scared, he raised himself to a sitting posture, and waited another minute, for he was scarcely yet fully awake.

At that instant, a flashing meteor described an arc in the sky, then disappeared into the sea. The constellations were brilliant. The Pleiades, the seven lovely daughters of Old Atlas, had by this time neared the zenith,

with Orion the Hunter in full pursuit, while
Sirius, the Dog-star, followed in its master's
steps.

At another time he would have turned his
scout's telescope upon them, but just then the
sound which had disturbed his rest began once
more. Again he listened breathlessly for a
few seconds, then realizing all at once what it
was, he sprang to his feet, and in one bound
he was bending close down to the receiver of
the "baby-wireless," which he had rigged up
only the day before, from the top of the ruined
tower down to a peg in the ground a few feet
away. Some message had been picked up by
the little instrument. Though he knew it not
as yet, it was the message for which all Europe
was listening at that moment.

He was a keen "wireless" student, although
an amateur. Placing the receiver close to his
ear, he waited for a repetition of the sounds.
He had not long to wait. It was a message of
but three words, and it came over the sea from
the Nord-Deutsch-Lloyd Wireless Station, but
it was destined to plunge ten nations into war,
to destroy millions of lives, and to cost thousands of millions of money.

"Zur-zip-zur, zip-zur-zip, zip-zip!" cried the instrument, giving up its secret.

"KRIEG IST ERKLAREN!"

"More beastly German!" exclaimed Danby in disgust, repeating the words over and over again, half-aloud; "and I don't understand a word of it. Poof! How I wish I had learnt German instead of French, then I might have understood this message."

Danby was totally unconscious of a movement close behind him, so intent was he upon the ticking instrument, until he felt a gentle touch upon his arm, when, turning, he came face to face with the scout-master, in whose voice there was just a touch of excitement as he said:—

"Krieg ist erklaren! Are you sure that is the message, my lad?"

"Yes, sir! I have had it three times. Can you tell me what it means?"

"War is declared! That's what it means!" replied John Holland, seriously. "War between England and Germany!"

CHAPTER II.

WAR IS DECLARED.

"War is declared?" exclaimed Danby in amazement, looking up into the serious face of the scout-master.

"Yes, that is the message, if you have recorded it correctly," replied Holland. "Let me listen a moment—not that I doubt you, for you are the most expert wireless man in the patrol, but I should like to make doubly certain."

"Here it comes again, sir!"

John Holland knelt upon the grass, took the receiver and placed it to his ear. Then he listened attentively, until the message had been repeated twice.

"You are right, Danby! War has been declared between England and Germany, and this message is being flashed, not only over Germany, but across the seas, so that every German ship within a thousand miles may pick

(19)

it up and run for some neutral port to avoid capture by the British cruisers, which, undoubtedly, by this time are already on their track."

"That is bad news, sir," exclaimed the youth, noting the tone of grave anxiety in which his leader spoke. He did not know what else to say, for he was bewildered and excited inwardly, though not a little proud of his success in thus tapping the enemy's wireless message.

"It is the worst news that ever travelled across the seas, either by cable or wireless, and yet England could not have acted otherwise and retained her honour. Thank God! It is better to die honourably than to live in dishonour."

"Shall I wake the patrol, sir?" asked Danby, who was not a little eager to communicate the great tidings.

"Not yet; let them sleep a little while longer, for they were very tired last night. I'll give you the tip for the reveille shortly; it will be earlier than usual. I want to think matters over a little before daybreak. Meanwhile, as England is at war, we must post sentries, and you'd better take the first watch from now till reveille," said John Holland.

"Yes, sir," answered the eager youth, and immediately he took up his post on the edge of the camp.

Then, while the proud Oscar kept watch over the silent camp, John Holland, deep in meditation, sauntered off along the edge of the cliff. Within ten minutes he was challenged by a coast-guard patrol, who was armed with a service rifle. Fortunately, he was recognized by the man who belonged to the adjoining station, and who only the previous day had been in the scouts' camp.

Here, however, was a speedy confirmation of the message which Danby's "toy-wireless" had picked up. The coast-guard officials had already received the news by telephone from head-quarters, and every mile of the East Coast was now being patrolled by armed parties.

As he returned to camp some hours later, Holland was again challenged, this time by the vigilant, keen-eyed Danby, who cried :—

"Halt! Who goes there?" in sharp, short tones, which roused half the camp, and made them rub their eyes with amazement.

"Friend!" replied the scout-master.

"Advance, friend, and give the password!" cried Danby, waking the rest of the camp.

"Be prepared!" came the reply in quiet tones.

"Pass, friend! All's well!" came the answer, for the scout's motto had been arranged as password till daybreak.

The dawn was just beginning to break. Towards the sunrising, a faint yellow streak lit up the sea, disclosing two destroyers with long trails of black smoke, low down upon the horizon. Next, a saffron tint flushed the edge of sky and sea, then spread rapidly. The stars faded and disappeared as the gates of the morning were unbarred. A hundred streamers of flashing roseate hue flooded the blue vault of heaven, and from a misty grey the wide expanse of troubled waters beneath changed to a pale green.

The owls and bats ceased their nocturnal vigil, and fled to some place of refuge, but the starlings came out of the cracks and crevices of the old ruined tower, which overlooked the Garden of Sleep, so long famous in story and song, and began to pipe and twitter, welcoming the morning sun. Up there in the azure, a lark was already pouring out a flood of melody, while the pleasant hum of insects told where the bees were already haunting the red poppies that covered half the cliffs. And as the dark curtain of night rolled westward, it marked the end of an age of luxury and peace, for THE DAY had come, and England was to be tried once again by blood and fire.

"Let Murphy sound the reveille," the scout-master ordered, directly he had entered the camp.

"Aye, aye, sir!"

Half a minute later, as the stirring notes of the reveille rang over the sea, the whole camp was astir with life and movement. The news of the war which had broken out passed rapidly from scout to scout, and formed the only subject of conversation. Every member of the patrol, with blazing eyes and eager speech, told his chum that he meant to enlist at once in the King's Army, in order that he might serve his country.

Murphy, whose father was a major in the Dublin Fusiliers, promised to write to his pater that very day on behalf of the others.

For one and all declared that even the post of drummer-boy in that or any other regiment just now, would be the very height of glory.

"And tell your pater, Murphy, that we are 'dab hands' at signalling, both with the flag and with the Morse code. That should help things on a bit!" exclaimed Bancroft.

"Say we want to join at once, Murphy," cried MacGregor, whose uncle was once in the Gordon Highlanders. "At once, mind ye, or else I'll go an' join the kilties the noo! Ye'll no' forget, Murphy?"

"No, it's meself'll do et at once, an' I'll not forget it, MacGregor, but the kilties are not to be compared to the Dublin Fusiliers, man."

A short blast on the scout-master's whistle produced instant silence, and stopped this friendly rivalry as to the merits of the various regiments in the British Army.

"Fall in! 'Shun! Right dress! Number!" came the orders in rapid sequence, and the whole squad responded smartly, toeing an invisible line as straight as a ruler.

Danby, the patrol-leader, called the roll, and reported to the chief—

"All present, sir! The Eagle Patrol is complete!" Then saluting, he took his place at the end of the line, ready for the morning observance of the flag salute.

"Patrol . . . Flag Salute . . . !" cried Holland.

Once more the bugle rang out, and as the rest of the patrol brought their right hands to the salute, Danby, by a dexterous movement hoisted the Union Jack upon their telescopic mast. Then, as the morning breeze flung out the folds of the old flag, round upon round of cheers greeted this emblem of the British nation. Never before had these lads felt such ringing pride and enthusiasm over that piece of coloured bunting. At that moment, there was not a youth in the patrol who would not have given his life for that flag.

John Holland stepped forward to address them, for his heart had been strangely stirred by this spontaneous outburst, but, seeing the light that shone in his eyes, the cheering commenced again, so that for some minutes it was impossible for the scout-master to be heard. For once, it seemed as though the discipline of the patrol was endangered, but one short blast of the whistle, however, restored instant silence and obedience.

"Lads of the Eagle Patrol," began the chief, "yesterday we were at peace with the whole world; to-day we are at war! Seventy-five years ago, England signed a treaty along with France and Germany which guaranteed that little Belgium should be protected against invasion by any greedy neighbour who desired her territory. Yesterday came the news that, despite this treaty, the German legions had crossed the border, and were burning the villages of Belgium, shooting down the peasantry who resisted, and committing acts of violation and treachery unheard of before in all the history of civilization. We knew yesterday, therefore, that we were on the brink of a terrible war unless this reign of terror ceased and the Germans withdrew.

"Yesterday, Belgium appealed to us, the people of England, to save her from the despoiling hand of the tyrant, and, without hesitation, the British Government cried to Germany across the cables :—

"'Hands off Belgium! Withdraw your legions or we shall unsheathe the sword! We

will not stand idly by, and by our silence consent to this great evil!'"

Here it was impossible for the scout-master
to proceed, for at this point his speech was
punctuated by wild and almost frantic cheers.
When at length silence had been restored,
John Holland continued :—

"England cannot break her word; it is her
bond! Justice and honour demanded that unless the bully withdrew, the whole might of the
British Empire should be hurled against the
tyrant. Yesterday afternoon, there was just a
hope amongst some of us that Germany would
withdraw and compensate Belgium for thus
tearing up a treaty, which was seventy-five
years old, and had always been respected before, but to-day even that spark of hope has
been extinguished, and England has perforce
been compelled to declare war. You may
wonder how I know this, seeing that the
morning papers have not yet arrived, but last
night your patrol-leader himself picked up a
message on his 'toy-wireless' from over the
sea, which told us the news; in addition I have
this morning seen the coast-guard and they have
informed me that war has been declared."

"Bravo, Danby, Bravo!" shouted the lads, who were now in a mood to cheer at anything almost, so that it needed all Danby's authority as patrol-leader to prevent himself being carried shoulder high round the camp.

Then the patrol was dismissed, amid a buzz of excitement and enthusiasm, John Holland signifying that he was going to the village for news, and afterwards, at the morning parade, he might have something further to say about this momentous event. So the lads scattered, racing down the steep hillside to the beach, in order to enjoy their morning swim in the breakers, which was usually followed by a sun-bath and races on the sands below.

CHAPTER III.

" SCHMIDT."

" COME along, Bancroft, Willoughby, all of you, let's have a swim out to the mark-buoy and back again," cried Danby.

" Agreed!" they all shouted, for swimming was but second nature to the Eagles.

" Your turn to be starter, Willoughby, though, is it not ? "

" Yes, sir," replied the latter somewhat crest-fallen, " I—I think it is."

" Well, we'll have a second race, and you shall come into that. Here . . . toe the line you fellows . . . usual handicaps, and ten points to the winner towards the new shield."

" All ready ? " called Willoughby, catching up some of his lost enthusiasm, as he saw the clean-limbed youths toe the long line on the sand, straining to get away like hounds on the leash.

" Yes, all ready ! " they replied.

"Away, Eagles! One, two, three, . . . twenty!" and away they went, Murphy and Shackleton starting together at one, Bancroft at seven, and so on till Danby himself, the scratch man, started at twenty.

Oh, the excitement and enthusiasm of that early morning race and swim! Willoughby, the only spectator on the beach, danced and capered about, hallooing, clapping his hands and shouting :—

"Go it, Murphy! Bravo, Shackleton!" his natural sympathy as usual being with the juniors, as he happened to be the smallest lad in the patrol.

Away they went like hounds unleashed, fairly sprinting over the yellow sand, splashing through the shallow water, then taking a header into the first breaker that came along, and, re-appearing on the surface, they struck out with all the ardour of strong and daring swimmers.

The mark-buoy was a hundred yards out from the edge of the water. Murphy was the first to round it, and Shackleton followed within five seconds, the rest all in a cluster, save Danby, who had given the others a long start.

"Stick it, Murphy! Stick it!" cried Wil-

loughby, as he thought he saw his favourite
flag a little when half-way back.

At that moment, Danby, coming up with the
"overhand stroke," was passing one after
another, until towards the end the race seemed
to be between Murphy and Danby. Then it
was that the cheering started afresh, not only
from Willoughby, but from those of the Eagles
who had been passed, who had spirit enough to
cheer little Murphy—he, it seemed, had still a
sporting chance. Even the vigilant coast-guard,
patrolling the cliff-top, found time for a moment to watch the Eagles, and, half a mile
away, a company of Engineers who had come
down in fast motor-cars to plan out the East
Coast entrenchments looked on through their
glasses.

Murphy touched land first, then splashing
once more through the shallow water, he
scrambled to his feet, followed closely by
Danby; then came the final sprint across the
sand to the mark, where Willoughby stood,
frantically waving a towel, and still urging on
the resolute Murphy, by such words as :—

"Well done, Murphy! Bravo, young Eagle!"
so that Danby, who was putting on speed, and

in another two seconds would have outpaced the youngster, could not find it in his heart to outstrip the lad, and so, easing down just a wee trifle, that was hardly discernible, the two came in together, receiving as much of an ovation as the rest of the Eagles, being now puffed and blown, could manage to give.

Thus ended the morning race ; which was followed by a few others, short ones, at varying intervals, and also beach races and a sunbath. Then the Eagles dressed and climbed back to the camp, ready for the breakfast parade. Was it any wonder that these lion's cubs were strong and resolute, both morally and physically, for experts will have it that the cold bath and vigorous towelling is both a moral and a physical tonic.

If the Eagles were not heroes, they were at any rate made of the stuff of which heroes are made. They only needed the opportunity to do brave deeds, and though they knew it not as yet, the time was rapidly approaching when every one of them would be tested to the utmost. Within another twelve months they were to win undying fame on the great battlefield of Europe, though the sad day must yet come when an English General would speak of them as

"'THE LOST PATROL,'

"who rendered valiant service to the cause of England."

Just as they were assembling for breakfast John Holland returned from the village, and his countenance was still very grave.

"Lads," he said, "the news is very serious. Fighting has begun already around Liège and Visé. The French are also fighting in Alsace and Lorraine, for the Germans have also crossed the border there, or tried to.

"I wish that you were all a couple of years older," went on the master. "Willoughby there is only fifteen, and even Danby is but a trifle over sixteen, though you are all big, strong youths for your age. Nevertheless, the British Government does not accept men for the colours till they are eighteen."

"What if we had been eighteen, sir?" asked one of the scouts.

"Then we could all have joined some regiment together, for, I am convinced of this, that in the coming struggle England will need

3

every able-bodied man who can carry a rifle, to defend her cause against the tyrant."

"But some of us are big enough for Guardsmen, sir," broke in one of the lads. "Bancroft is five feet nine, and Danby is five feet ten!"

"Most of us are tall enough, sir. It's only Willoughby who would be left behind!" urged another.

"What? Leave me behind?" said Willoughby in a choking voice, and with the tears glistening in his eyes. "I won't be left behind. I will go and enlist now . . . now!" he exclaimed in a voice that betokened both anger and tears.

"Wait just a wee bit longer, lads, and I believe in my heart that a chance will come for all of us, perhaps even Willoughby included. And if it were possible for me to take the whole patrol to the front, attached to some regiment or brigade . . . well, I should be the happiest man in all England, but I am afraid that the authorities will not listen to us, though, I tell you plainly, I mean to try them."

"Bravo! Three cheers for the scout-master!" cried some one, and again a volley of cheers went up along with a number of hats.

"You must remember, however," continued Holland, "that you are as yet all juniors, and the sanction of your parents will be necessary to whatever steps you take in the matter, though I believe you will have little trouble on that score. Besides, it is just possible that, considering the flattering words of the Chief-Scout, when he highly commended the Eagle Patrol at our last Rally at Windsor Castle, that some notice might be taken of our application at head-quarters. At any rate, you may leave the matter in my hands for a few days, and I will do my best.

"And now, lads, to breakfast! Sound the 'Cook-house,' Murphy!"

The Eagles were just sitting down to breakfast on the green sward at the cliff-top, when some one remarked :—

"Hullo, where's Willoughby? He's missing! Where can he have gone?"

"Willoughby missing?" cried the chief. "Did any one see him leave the camp?"

"No, sir," cried several voices.

"He was here ten minutes ago," said Murphy.

"Did he say anything about leaving the camp?" asked the scout-master.

"No, sir. He only seemed a trifle unhappy about being left behind, if the patrol should go to the front."

"Perhaps he's really gone to enlist as he said he would," suggested some one.

"It's very strange. . . . I've never known any of you to leave camp before without permission, least of all would I have suspected Willoughby," said the chief somewhat sternly. Then, turning to Murphy, he ordered :—

"Sound the 'Breakfast-call' again, bugler! And scatter around, the rest of you ; he can't be far away."

For the next ten minutes there was no thought of the breakfast which was fast spoiling. The lads searched high and low in the vicinity of the camp for the absentee. Every hollow was examined by the ubiquitous scouts ; every tree, shrub and bush explored. But no trace of Willoughby could be found anywhere.

Then the bugler was ordered to sound the "Fall In" in the hope that the straggler, hearing the call, might be brought to a sense

of honour, and join the assembly with the rest.
For, should he not, then was he liable to be
treated as a deserter, and expelled from the
patrol.

There was still no sign of the missing lad,
and John Holland requested Murphy to sound
the "Assembly" a second time to give the lad
another chance.

Scarcely had the last notes of the bugle-call
died away, when there came the well-known
signal of distress from a scout's whistle a
quarter of a mile away. This was followed
quickly by a pistol shot.

"Patrol . . . Quick March . . . Double!"
came the instantaneous order.

As the lads started off smartly, they could
hear the chief telling Danby, who was close
beside him in the race, that there was some
mischief afoot, and he feared they might be
too late. A moment later Danby himself
cried out :—

"See . . . the coast-guard wires are cut.
There must be a German spy!"

CHAPTER IV.

THE SPY-HUNT.

As Danby uttered these words, the others noticed that just ahead of them the telephone wires which ran along the edge of the cliff had been cut, and were dangling upon the ground. But what thrilled them most of all was the sight of poor young Willoughby, lying unconscious upon the very edge of the cliff, which at this spot was very steep and precipitous. Evidently he had left the camp unnoticed, after having announced his intention to enlist, and had interrupted the spy at his nefarious work.   There were evident signs of a struggle.

As they picked him up, they saw that he was bleeding freely, and his scout's shirt was also torn.

"Look, he has been shot through the arm, sir!" exclaimed Shackleton.

Holland and Danby, who came racing up together, were already rendering first aid.

(38)

The sleeve of the shirt was removed; the wound was quickly dressed and bandaged, and a couple of rude splints were made. Then a rough stretcher made of two scout poles and a shirt with the sleeves turned inside out, and the poles threaded through, was soon arranged. This was but a matter of a couple of minutes.

"Do you think he is badly hurt, sir?" asked Danby.

"No, it's only a flesh wound, and not very dangerous," replied the scout-master. "He has fainted from loss of blood, but he'll soon recover."

"Willoughby! Willoughby!" called the chief. "Are you hurt much?"

Slowly, very slowly, the injured lad opened his eyes, looked wearily around, then closed them again, while a faint but sickly smile came over his pallid face.

"Bring a little sea-water, one of you, quickly, to wash these blood-stains away, and to cool his face. It may help to revive him."

At these words, MacGregor started away down a very steep pathway which led from the brink of the cliff to the shore, and while he was gone, John Holland said :—

"Did any of you see the man?"

"Yes, sir. I saw him!" cried Bancroft.

"Where?"

"At least, I saw a man running off as I came up. I was a little further to the left than the rest of you, and had to get round a bad gap in the cliff. As I did so, a man started up from behind the shrub over there, and walked swiftly past me. He had a golf club in his hand, and appeared to have been searching for a lost ball, so that I did not associate him with this affair. But when I looked back over my shoulder a few seconds later, I saw him running as hard as he could pelt."

"In which direction, Bancroft?"

"In the direction of Trimingham Gap, sir."

"Did you see his face?"

"Only for an instant, sir," replied Bancroft.

"Could you recognize him again?" asked the scout-master.

"I think I could. It was a clean-cut face, with an ugly scar on the left cheek. I could easily recognize his clothes, sir, for he wore a Norfolk coat and breeches of brown tweed."

"It strikes me that you've got a pretty fair

clue," said John Holland. "The Germans are
fond of duelling, and the scar on his cheek
might easily be the result of a duel. You and
Bancroft had better follow him up. Shadow
him if you can and we'll follow you up, as
soon as I've seen Willoughby brought round,
and reported the matter to the coast-guard."

"Aye, aye, sir!" replied Danby and Bancroft, and, without another moment's hesitation, they started away on this novel spy-hunt.

"Be on your guard!" shouted Holland.
"The man evidently carries a revolver."

So whilst Willoughby was carried on the
rough stretcher to the village by the other
lads, and placed under medical supervision,
the scout-master went direct to the coast-guard
station and reported the occurrence to the
chief petty officer in charge there.

Willoughby's wound proved, as John Holland had said, to be only a flesh wound. He
was sent by the doctor to the cottage hospital
a mile away.

"He'll be all right in a few days," said the
doctor, "and fit to join his patrol again. I'll
visit him every day, and see that he gets proper attention."

Meanwhile, let us follow Danby and Bancroft, as they make a bee-line over the sand-hills, the scrub and the dingles for Trimingham Gap. This was their first bit of real warfare And their spirits rose higher and higher as they told each other again and again that it was a real spy they were after this time; a spy who had already shot a member of their patrol.

"Bravo, little Willoughby!" said Bancroft. "If he's only five feet one, he's got the pluck of a guardsman, to tackle that fellow single-handed."

"Yes, plucky little rascal, there'll be no further talk of leaving him behind, now he's shown himself to be the real thing," replied the patrol-leader.

"But if I'd only known that the fellow who passed me with the golf club was the very devil who shot our young Eagle, I'd never have let him pass me like that."

"You think you'll know him, Bancroft, if we cross his path?" queried the other.

"Yes, I'd know him amongst a thousand."

It was rough going through all that gorse, prickly weeds, stinging nettles, and dry, long-

tufted grass.   But up hill and down dale they
never stopped their steady trot, though they
soon had to give up conversing, and save their
breath.   At last they reached the top of the
knoll close by the Gap and overlooking it.   It
was just one of those ordinary, sandy gullies
where a cleft in the hills allowed an approach
to the beach for cattle and vehicles, and which
are so common on the East Coast, especially
in Norfolk and Lincolnshire.

"There's the Gap at last!" exclaimed
Danby, who, though now quite breathless, had
cantered up the last slope a few yards in front
of his chum.

"Better not show ourselves over the ridge,
though.   If the rascal's got a hiding-place
there, he may be watching, and that will give
him time to make another spurt.   How do you
feel, Bancroft?"

"A little pumped, old man, that's all!" replied the second scout, as he sank down on the
landward slope of the down and lay flat for a
minute.

"That was a cross-country gallop and no
mistake.   We've done two miles at least of
that rough ground in sixteen minutes.   Beats

our hurdle race last May at Cockfosters, eh, old fellow?"

"You're about right, Danby, an' we're still on the wrong side of our breakfast."

"We'd better get our wind here for a couple of minutes, and, by Jove, but we're in luck's way. I've got a couple of bars of good plain chocolate here."

"Hooray! Thanks awfully!" exclaimed Bancroft, as Danby threw him a bar, and they both commenced to eat.

Five minutes afterwards, Danby crept to the top of the slope, and, using his little telescope, he peered carefully over the grassy summit of the hill, and searched the Gap for any sign of human being.

"Anything?" queried his chum, eagerly.

"Not a sign of any living thing. Not the slightest movement anywhere."

"Bad luck! Let me have a peep through your glass, old fellow, when you've finished."

Danby had another good look around, then handed the telescope to Bancroft, saying:—

"Just have a look at that little tuft of grass on the other slope there, by that broken fence, and tell me if you can see any movement."

Bancroft took the glass and scrutinized the spot closely for a full minute without speaking.

"Can you see anything?" asked Danby getting impatient.

"Nothing, except a little bit of paper blowing about with the breeze. Shall I go and get it? It might prove to be a lost letter which will give us a clue."

"Yes, go and get it, while I speak to this fisherman bringing his shrimp nets down the track which leads to the Gap."

Bancroft was over the hill-top and sliding down the smooth, velvety seaward slope within ten seconds, while his comrade took the path which would bring him out by the fisherman, as he came up.

"Good morning, sir!" said Danby politely to the old salt.

"Good morning, mi' lad! Would you loike a few fine shrimps for your breakfast, young measter?"

"Yes, that I would indeed!" replied the lad, who was now as hungry as a hunter, seeing that, though it was not yet seven o'clock in the morning, he had spent nearly three hours in the open air, with only a bar of chocolate to eat.

"Then come with me, young measter, an' ye shall have your capful within half an hour, all ready for bilin'."

Danby shrugged his shoulders, but declined the old man's invitation gracefully, saying that he was on patrol duty, or he would have come gladly.

"Mebbe you're watchin' for these Garmans as be a-comin' to land here soon!" ventured the fisherman with a smile, as he prepared to walk on.

"Stop a minute, sir!" cried the youth. "You haven't met anyone on the road, I suppose, as you came from the village this morning?"

"Met anyone, did you say, measter? Why, yes, I did meet a stranger a-comin' from the beach, or mebbe from the golf links. Why do you ask?"

"How was he dressed, sir?" asked Danby eagerly, ignoring the latter part of the man's speech.

The old man stopped short, pulled off his hat and began to scratch his head. Then he began slowly :—

"Why, let me see now, he were wearin' a

brown tweed suit an' breeches, like as these gentry wear who come fra' Lunnon an' play golf here. It be foine bracing air this for the Lunnon folk, who always live in the fog," went on the garrulous old fellow, slipping away from the subject.

" And did he carry a golf club, sir ? " queried Danby, getting excited, but bringing the stranger back to the point.

" Why, yes, I think he did. He couldn't play golf without one, could he, young measter ? " replied the old man with just a twinkle in his eyes.

" Thank you very much. I want to catch him up before he gets too far away."

" He be your faither, I 'spect, down from Lunnon, an' you want to catch him afore he gets to Trimingham Station, eh ? " chuckled the old man. " Mebbe he forgot to leave ye your week's spending money, young measter ! "

Danby could scarcely repress a smile at the old man's innocent joke, and stayed only just long enough to put another question to the fisherman.

" Was he going to Trimingham Station, sir ? "

"You baint quarrelled with the old 'un, hev ye?" said the stranger facetiously.

The scout laughed, but repeated the question, and the other replied :—

"Well, he was agoin' in that direction, but he never replied to me when I bid him ' Good mornin',' so I let him go by, but ye'll have to 'urry up if ye're agoin' to catch him."

"Thank you, sir. A thousand thanks!" said Danby, just then catching sight of Bancroft, to whom he gave a signal with his extended arm.

CHAPTER V.

THE ESCAPE.

Half a minute later Bancroft came up at a sprint, and the two scouts started at a good pace in the direction of Trimingham, leaving the old man to his shrimping nets.

"What do you think, Banky?" said Oscar, as soon as they were out of earshot. "The Allemande is only ten minutes ahead of us!"

"No, really?" exclaimed the other in surprise. "You don't mean it?"

"Yes," replied Danby. "That old man with the shrimp net met him going in the direction of Trimingham as he came down to the Gap just now."

"Then we're in luck's way. Let's do a sprint to the next turn in the road; we may catch sight of him."

"Right ho!"

So they started off again, not exactly at a

sprint, but at a good jog trot, and as they ran side by side, Danby said to his chum :—

"Garrulous old fellow, wasn't he ? but what a pleasant round face he'd got. Should love to have gone shrimping and prawning with him this morning. He offered to get me a capful for breakfast within half an hour, but he would take this cursed Allemande for my pater."

"Would he, indeed ? " laughed Bancroft. "That explains, then, what he said to me as I passed him coming up."

"What did he say ? "

"Why, he evidently noticed this lasso coiled on to my shoulder-strap, and just as I passed he called out to me :—

"'Hey, you baint agoin' to hang the old man when you ketch him, are you ?'"

Both the scouts laughed heartily at this, and Danby added :—

"We may even have to do that yet if he whips out his pistol to us. It's a stroke of luck that you brought the lasso down to the camp, especially as you are such an expert man with it. Could you land him with it at twenty yards, do you think ? "

"I'd have a jolly good try, anyhow, if he showed fight."

As they jogged along, Danby, every now and then, remembering that the patrol were to follow in their steps, marked a tree or a fence with an arrow giving the direction. When he came to a cross-road he would also give the sign, so well known to the Eagles, that a certain path was not to be taken. This was a rude cross with a semblance to the flag of St Andrew.

If any other scout signs were observed anywhere, then Danby would give a rough sketch of the head of an eagle, in addition ; the sign which was so familiar to every member of the troop. With these marks to guide him, even a tenderfoot could not have missed the way ; for the Eagles who were following, it was like reading an open book.

They reached the turn in the road at length, but nothing appeared in view, so on they went. They were not very far from Trimingham now, where there is a little station on the coast railway which runs from Holt to North Walsham. Now they dropped their gait to a steady walking pace, keeping their eyes and ears open. Then they fell to speculating as to why the spy had taken this route, and what his intention could be.

" He cannot be far ahead of us now, unless he has run all the way," exclaimed Danby.

" Which isn't likely. He didn't look it, and if he had sprinted two hundred yards with that ' bierbauch' he would have been puffed. I tell you he didn't look like a man in training, so he can't be far ahead of us."

" It would be unfortunate, though, should he just catch a train leaving Trimingham as we came up."

" I should be shivering mad if he did. I wonder if there is a train so early in the morning."

" It's quite likely that he's arranged it all very neatly, so as to cut the wires and just get away. The Germans are such brutes for organizing all the petty details," replied Danby.

" Then we'd better put up another canter. The village and station cannot be more than three-quarters of a mile from here. The next bend in the road will bring them both into view. I came down here for the chief last Saturday to fetch some of his luggage."

" Listen, Bancroft ! Did you hear that ? "

" Yes, I heard it. Hey, presto ! Let's gallop ! " and gallop they did, for the sound which they had both heard was the shriek of a locomotive. Whether it was a train entering or leaving the station they could not tell, nor did they stop to argue. They just did one of their " eleven seconds per hundred " sprints to the bend which was but a hundred and twenty yards away. As they rounded the corner they could see the village clearly within twelve minutes' walk, but what distressed them most of all was a long cloud of white steam from a passenger train.

" Too late ! " gasped the patrol-leader, easing down to get breath, after the sharp sprint.

" I fear so. The rascal has escaped us."

" He has timed it so well that no one could follow him."

" Wait a minute, though, we'll do it after all ! " cried Bancroft, springing to his feet again, for he had thrown himself down on the grassy bank by the roadside for a moment, but, looking once more in the direction of the railway, he leapt back into the road and pointed towards Trimingham.

"Well, what do you make of that?" said Danby, following with his eyes the direction pointed out by his chum, and wondering what had possessed him.

"See . . . the steam has been shut off. The train is only just entering the station. It whistled at the level crossing. I remember now, the station is behind that windmill over there."

For answer, Danby gave a long, low whistle, then exclaimed :—

"By Jove, Banky, you're right! I believe we'll do it after all. At any rate, there is just a sporting chance. Come on!" and away they went like the wind.

Down the road they peltered. It was only half a mile. Could they do it? The train was in the station now. How long would it remain there? Oh, if by chance, it would only remain there four or five minutes, they might just catch it after all. In their boyish enthusiasm they did not stop to think that even if they reached the station before the train started, it would be necessary to search the compartments to discover if the suspected spy was aboard. And even if they found him, what were they going to do? They could not charge him without offering some evidence. They did not think of all these things. In their own minds, however, he was the spy who had cut the wires and shot Willoughby, although they had seen him do neither.

The train had not started yet, although they were just entering the village. Down the deserted street they tore as if pursued by a mad bull. Their faces were almost as red as fire with the heat and exercise, while the perspiration stood in great beads on their foreheads. They were also showing signs of fag, and no wonder, after all their exercise and excitement. Still they kept on, for their hearts were just as resolute as their bodies and limbs were sturdy and strong.

They were almost at the station now, within fifty yards of the open fence that skirted the tiny platform, when—

"Shriek! Puff—Puff!" came the sound of the starting engine, and they now knew for certain that they were too late.

In spite of this bad fortune, they both dashed at the little wicket gate, but found it had been clicked to, and, as it locked auto-

matically, they were left outside, for the soli-
tary man who served as ticket-collector, porter
and station-master, at this early hour, was
away at the other end of the platform, throwing the last bundle of parcels into the guard's
van.

At another time this slight barrier of a five-
foot gate and railing would not have debarred
them for ten seconds. As it was Danby tried
to clear it, but he fell back again, and gave it
up. They were both too utterly fagged to
clear the obstacle, and all they could do was
to lean for support on the rail, as the train
passed by within five yards of them.

"There he is!" gasped Bancroft, as the last
compartment vanished past them.

And for a moment both the lads got a
glimpse of a hard, cruel face at the window,
which, however, withdrew immediately behind
the half-drawn curtain, the instant he saw the
scouts.

"Did you see him, Danby?" gasped Bancroft, half-choking with rage and disappointment.

"Yes, I saw him, and I shall know him
again!"

"Heavens! to think he's escaped us after all this fag. I feel as if I could die with grief," exclaimed the lad.

"Don't do that, Banky, old fellow! We haven't lost him yet. It's a pity you gave us away by shouting out just now."

"I couldn't help it! To think the 'varmint' has got clean away."

"Not yet!" replied Danby. "Come with me, and I'll show you the next move."

Bancroft followed his patrol-leader, crushed by a sense of disappointment at their failure. It was their first real spy-hunt, and they had failed through no fault of their own. Circumstances had been dead against them.

"Another minute, Danby, and we should have landed him, for I am certain now that he was the man we want," said Bancroft in a tone of bitterness.

"Cheer up, old boy. We'll have him yet or I'm very much mistaken. We have identified our man, at any rate," replied Danby.

"Yes. Did you notice the scar on his cheek?"

"I did, and in addition, I noted the look of

alarm on his face when we appeared suddenly at the gate."

"Where are you going to now?"

"I'm going to wire to Mundesley. Come along, there's no time to lose."

CHAPTER VI.

CLOSING THE NET.

DANBY had noticed two strands of wire that stretched across the street to a private house close by. He hesitated for a moment. Should he ask permission to 'phone from that house? It seemed to be the only telephone in the vicinity, unless he walked up the line to the nearest signal-box, and that would be wasting time. His mind was made up quickly.

"Come along, Bancroft," he said. "This is our next move. The train will be at Mundesley in about eight minutes." Then he walked over to where a portly gentleman, in carpet slippers and a smoking jacket, was puffing away at a pipe by the little garden gate.

"Good morning, sir!" began Danby, saluting.

"Good morning, Sonny! I see you've lost the train. But cheer up, there'll be another in two hours and a half."

The patrol-leader smiled suavely, and wondered whether all the people on the East Coast were as facetious as the old salt. This seemed to be another sample of them, at any rate.

"Well, sir," he began, "I didn't want to catch the train. I wanted to catch somebody on the train."

"Oh, not the gentleman with the golf sticks, I suppose? He nearly missed it; seemed mighty flurried too. Hardly like an Englishman."

"Yes, sir, that was the gentleman I desired to catch. May I trouble you to let me use your 'phone, so that I may speak to Mundesley?"

"Why—oh, certainly! Step inside. Nothing wrong, I hope? No one seriously ill?"

"Well, it is something rather serious."

"Here's the telephone. What number do you want?"

"I want the Police Station, Mundesley, if you please," said Danby.

"Eh, what's that? The Police Station, did you say?"

"Yes, sir. We mustn't waste time. We

fear that gentleman is the spy who cut the coast-guard wires this morning, and also shot one of our troop, a lad of fifteen."

"Eh, what? The devil he did! Then he is a German spy, the hound!"

"We are afraid so. Have you got the number, Bancroft?" asked Danby of his chum, who was fumbling with the telephone directory.

"Never mind the number, lad. Ask for the Police Station, Mundesley, and they'll give it to you at once," said the old man eagerly.

"Thank you, sir!"

"Hullo! Hullo! Are you there?"

"Yes. Who do you want?" asked the Exchange.

Two minutes later, the police at Mundesley had received the information, and had replied that the train would be duly met on arrival; it was not due for another three minutes, and the station was only a hundred yards away. The scouts were also asked to come on by the next train to identify the man and to lay the charge against him.

"Humph! if that rascal's arrested, you boys have done a grand day's work. Probably you've arrested the first German spy since war was declared. But, I say, how tired and fagged you look! Have you been up all night after the rascal?"

They laughed and told him briefly their adventures that morning, but he cut them short, saying :—

"And you haven't touched breakfast yet?"

"We had a bar of chocolate, sir, a little while ago," put in Danby.

"Bar of chocolate? What's a bar of chocolate for two lion's cubs like you, who've run all the way from Overstrand to Trimingham Gap, and from Trimingham Gap to here; not to mention a few races in the sea and on the beach?" With that the queer old gentleman pulled an ancient bell-rope, and, when the servant appeared, he said :—

"Mary, breakfast for two, an' enough for six, afore these young gentlemen faint!"

"Yes, sir," replied Mary, as she retired, smiling, to the kitchen.

The old man was as good as his word. He actually stood over the hungry cubs and made them eat until they were ashamed of themselves. When at length they had mastered four eggs apiece, with a couple of rashers of fried ham cut none too thin, and ample slices of bread, he let them slack off.

Six months afterwards, when they were both prisoners in Germany, hungry and famished for want of decent food, subsisting on a crust of bread and a basin of Kartoffel soup, they recalled this breakfast, and wished in their young hearts that they might breakfast with the good old Norfolk magistrate once again.

Before they had finished the meal, the telephone bell rang, and Mr. John Beadle, the magistrate, answered it. A moment later, he rushed back into the breakfast-room, shouting aloud :—

" The rascal has escaped ! "

" No, surely not ? " cried both the youths, springing to their feet.

" Yes, he never reached Mundesley ! "

" But you saw him leave yourself, sir, and Mundesley is the next stop ! "

" Yes, I know it is, but the guard of the train says some one left the train about half-way between the two stations. He called out to him, but he took no notice, and quickly disappeared over the embankment near a wood."

"Then we are right in suspecting him. He must be the wanted person, else why should he leave the train when in motion?" cried Bancroft.

"Yes, but here comes the rub," said the magistrate. "The man who left the train was not wearing a brown suit, but was dressed in shabby clothes. What do you think of that? Neither was he so big and stout as the golfer whom I saw depart from here by the seven-fourteen. How do you account for that, Mr. Sherlock Holmes?"

This seemed puzzling, and threw them off the scent for a while, until Danby said :—

"He must be a master-spy, a veritable contortionist, able to change his shape and appearance at will. He was alone in the compartment, and could easily change his clothes between the two stations."

" Yes, my boy, he is a master-spy, and he'll give you another run before you get him into the net. Then he'll turn dangerous and perhaps kill the lot of you. You've done your bit and you'd better let the matter rest now in other hands. The police are following the matter up, with the coast-guard, and General

Maxwell, I hear, who commands the Eastern Division, is expected down to-day."

The two Eagles demurred at this somewhat. Their blood was up. This scoundrel had wounded one of their patrol; the youngest lad of the six. Careless whether he was dead or alive, he had, moreover, left him unconscious on the very edge of the cliff; perhaps even had tried to throw him over, for there had been a scuffle. At all costs he must be run to earth, and as he was still less than three miles away, why should they not join in the spy-hunt?

" I see you mean to go on with it," laughed the magistrate; " well, you wouldn't be English boys if you didn't. But be careful . . . he'll prove a desperate character when you corner him."

While they were preparing to depart, a police motor drove up quickly, and stopped at the house of the magistrate. In it was the superintendent of police, an inspector, and two constables, in addition to a military officer.

They immediately asked for the boys, who gave them all the particulars they could furnish, thus relieving them from the necessity of

5

going on to Mundesley. At that moment, John
Holland and the other three Eagles also arrived
upon the scene. They had carried Willoughby
to safety ; reported the affair to the coast-guard ;
and had then followed the trail of the other
two Eagles to Trimingham.

As the police motor prepared to start again,
the scout-master stepped forward, and, handing
his card to the superintendent, asked if he
might be of any use in searching the neighbourhood with his patrol for the culprit.

" Certainly, by all means. They seem in-
telligent lads for their age. Let them search
the seaward side of the line from here to Mundesley. But be careful, this man has slipped
through our net before this. He is a dangerous and crafty foreigner. But there you are
. . . find him if you can, but be careful ! "

" Thank you, sir," replied Holland. Then,
seeing the motor just starting, he ordered :—

" Eagles . . . fall in ! 'Shun ! Eyes left ! "
and gave the authorities of the law a smart
salute as they went off. This, the superintendent acknowledged smiling, as he called back :—

" A smart patrol, sir ! "

" By the left, quick march ! " called the commandant, and so they left the village, waving a farewell to the kindly old magistrate.

"Now, lads," said John Holland, when they had marched a few hundred yards along the road that led out of the village, into the broken path that wound in and out behind the cliffs and sandhills, "we've got a task before us to find this man, but he can't be far away. The police as well as the military are now scouring the place for him. It's just possible we may lay him by the heels with a bit of first-class scouting. If we do, we shall be rendering a service of the first magnitude to the country, and, in addition, it may serve us in another way."

"Indeed, sir!" asked several of the boys. "In what way will it help us?"

"You remember this morning I spoke about taking the whole patrol to the front, if an opportunity occurred."

"Yes, sir, we remember!" cried several voices at once.

"Yes; well, now, if we could lay this clever spy by the heels, I believe the Government could not refuse our offer. They would most likely consent to attach us to some brigade.

and when that was moved to the front, we should probably move with it."

"Bravo! Then we'll catch him, if it can be done," cried MacGregor.

Soon afterwards a halt was made, and the whole group got under cover, in a little sandy dingle, near the cliffs. Here the plan of operation was drawn up for the day. The chief made each of them draw a rough copy of his map, with the roads, cross-roads, etc., and he also arranged the necessary signals. They were to scout two and two, and gradually advance, covering all the ground from the seaboard to the railway, which varied in width from a third to three-quarters of a mile.

In turning out his pockets for his pocketbook, Bancroft drew forth the slip of paper which he had picked up by the Gap, and which he had intended handing over to Danby the patrol-leader, but the excitement of the race for the train, and the long string of other occurrences which had subsequently taken place, had naturally caused him to forget all about it.

"Look, Danby!" he cried. "I wanted to show you this half-sheet of note-paper, which I picked up by the Gap this morning, but I have forgotten it till now."

"Anything in it?" queried Danby, who was already busy with his chart.

"No, only it struck me as curious. Where the fellow who wrote it learnt to make those funny tails I can't make out. Looks like old English, doesn't it?"

John Holland raised his head at these words, and said :—

"Let me see it, Bancroft, for a moment, please."

"Certainly, sir," and the sheet of paper was handed to him. The scout-master uttered a note of surprise immediately he saw it.

"This was written by a German, Bancroft!" he exclaimed.

"A German, sir? But it's written in plain English, and merely refers to somebody's aunt and uncle, and so on."

"Yes, but you misunderstand me. There is a touch of Gothic about these capital letters, which betrays the nationality of the man who wrote it. It was written by a German."

At these words, the Eagles looked at each other, and at their chief, in blank amazement.

The mystery seemed to deepen. What would be the end of it all?

"Snakes alive!" gasped Murphy, when at length he found utterance. "Just fancy the fellow dropping his correspondence into our hands like that."

"Hadn't we better be starting, sir, while the trail is hot?" urged one or two of the lads, showing just a little impatience, for they were very eager.

But for a couple of minutes the scout-master heeded them not, for he was wrestling with the secret of the mysterious letter which he held in his hand.

CHAPTER VII.

A CLEVER CAPTURE.

JOHN HOLLAND was a master of the German language. He had studied it at Heidelberg and Bonn, and had long taught it at the Old Grammar School. When, therefore, he took up the half-sheet of note-paper, and noted the Gothic touch about the capital letters, the secret was laid bare at once.

"It was written by a German!" he repeated, as the Eagles clustered about him, and examined the caligraphy.

"How long have you had it, Bancroft?" he asked.

"About a couple of hours, sir."

"And where did you say that you found it?"

"Near to Trimingham Gap, sir."

Then the scout-master held the paper up to the light and scrutinized it carefully.

"Ah, I thought so!" he exclaimed, after a

short pause. "Here is a message in German, written in invisible ink, and also a tiny sketch, resembling the coast-line. The man who lost this is a secret agent of the German Government, without doubt, and a more damning piece of evidence could not by any chance be used against him."

Naturally, the Eagles were filled with excitement. They wanted the chief to read the German, and unravel the mystery to them at once.

"That is not quite possible," he said, "for it is written in code, and without the key it will be impossible to do much with it, but the sketch of the coast-line may help us in directing our search to-day. Just go on with your maps, while I give ten minutes to unravelling as much of it as I can."

So for the next few minutes the scout-master sat apart, puzzling over the precious bit of paper which Bancroft had found, while the rest of the patrol went on with their topography. At the end of that time he got up and said :—

"Now then, Eagles, we must get to work at once. I have not done much to solve the riddle, but I have formed one or two new ideas as to our search."

Then he appointed the troop to their several stations. Now, the road which runs from Trimingham to Mundesley lies almost parallel with the railway and the coastline, and is pretty equidistant from the two; that is, it cuts the piece of terrain into two long strips. MacGregor and Shackleton were placed to the south towards the railway; Bancroft and Murphy were given the coast section, while Danby and the scout-master took the middle section, with the road generally as their centre. Every arrangement had been made for signalling, and it was ordered specially that each scout was to observe without being seen, as far as possible. Then the sweeping operations began.

Gradually, but thoroughly, every yard of the terrain was submitted to a close scrutiny. The Eagles were no novices at scouting, and, even if the Sherlock Holmes' at Scotland Yard had organized the sweep, it could not have been arranged any better. Fortunately, the Eagles had everything in their favour. The atmosphere was clear and the visibility was good. Every bit of scrub, every sandhill and dingle, every hedge and ditch was carefully explored ; while every now and then the scout-master, with his glasses, picked up the signal of an extended arm, or the wave of a flag, even from his furthest picket, which told him how things were progressing.

An hour passed—two hours, and it was getting towards noon, but as yet no discovery had been made, nor a suspicion aroused even, but the scouts with unwearied diligence continued the search.

Danby was now on the slope of Beacon Hill, which rises over two hundred feet above sea-level. It was here that his suspicions were first aroused. For the moment he was alone ; the scout-master, who had been acting closely on his left, had now gone over for a brief visit to the patrols on the left wing, in response to a flag-wave from Bancroft, who had evidently seen something.

During the last quarter of an hour Danby had made no advance, for he had been keenly watching the roadway from behind a piece of scrub. Here, he had a good view of the road for a considerable stretch, and he had noticed that one vehicle, which he had observed at a distance, had not yet appeared at the bend of the road, which at this point curves somewhat. Subsequent vehicles had already passed, and, from behind cover, he had carefully scrutinized every one and everything which had gone by.

"Where has that other vehicle gone?" he repeatedly asked himself. "It certainly has not passed me. I wonder now, if it can have turned in somewhere, through a gap?" he surmised. "I will wait another three minutes. and if the chief does not come back I will go forward alone."

The minutes passed slowly, but Holland did not return.

"H'm! it's a bit suspicious, at any rate, so here goes!" and with that Danby swung forward from cover to cover.

He had reached the slope of the next hillock, from which he expected a more extended view, when the neigh of a horse startled him, and he dropped down into the long grass for cover. Evidently that which he sought was on the reverse slope, or in the dingle at the bottom.

He listened carefully for a moment, then,

hearing no other sound, he crept slowly up the
hillock, like a snake through the grass.   When
he reached the summit he peeped carefully over.
Yes, there they were !   All that had aroused his
suspicions were there, just below, but Danby
could have rocked with laughter.   What a
mistake he had made !   Even a tenderfoot
would not have been so far misled.   There
was nothing but a pedlar of cheap wares, with
a wretched nag, hitched with broken-down
harness to a little, low cart, piled with cheap
tinware and crockery.

The owner and charioteer of this dismal
"turn-out" was as wretched-looking as his
nag, and now sat by a little fire cooking something for his midday meal ; a short, broken
clay pipe in his mouth.   The scout could not
see the man's face fully, for a wide, but broken-
brimmed hat half-hid it from view.

Danby's first thought was one of pity, and
he instinctively felt in his haversack for something which he might give to the pedlar to im-
prove his meal, but the haversack was empty ;
he had left the camp in too great a hurry to
fill it that morning.

Seeing no cause for further scrutiny, therefore, he was about to withdraw, when a long, low whistle, scarcely audible, reached his ears. The sound came from the other side of the gully, and immediately on hearing it the pedlar rose to his feet and made a signal with his hand. In doing so, his face caught the light more fully, as he looked warily around, and Danby saw a scar on his face that showed through all the dirt and grime. He also recognized the clean-cut features which he had seen in the train, despite the owner's attempt to disguise them.

"Heavens! It is the German spy!" gasped the youth, turning three shades paler all of a sudden.

As he looked on, spell-bound, wondering what the next turn would be, he saw another man, evidently an accomplice, come out of his cover, and step forward to meet the pedlar. For a moment Danby's heart beat rapidly, for they were only forty yards away. If he moved they would notice him, and they would quickly deal with him as with poor Willoughby, only perhaps more quietly.

What was he to do? It was on his mind to give the scream of an eagle, which was the rallying call of the patrol. But no, that would never do. The men would clear out rapidly, and the search would have to begin again. Besides, he very much doubted whether he could scream just now. His tongue seemed to be tied, and his very blood frozen. He had never been in such a tight corner before.

"Fritz, wie befinden sie sich?" exclaimed the pedlar.

"Sehr wohl, Ich danke, Carl. Sind sie fertig?"

Danby waited to hear no more. While they were thus engaged in their first greetings, he withdrew his head below the summit, and the shelter of the friendly bush, retreating a few paces backwards. Then he looked carefully around for help. None of the scouts were in view. What should he do? Should he go back and report? He would be sure to pick up some of the patrol within ten minutes. But in ten minutes many things might happen, and the trail might be lost. No, it was his duty to keep the men in view. They were dangerous spies, and at all costs he must keep them under observation. Some of the patrol would appear in view shortly, and then one signal from his hand would bring him assistance.

But oh, how slowly the minutes passed. Every one seemed like an hour. Twice he had crept back to look at the Germans, for his courage had returned, and a new light gleamed in his eyes. It was the hero within him re-asserting itself. Yet, though it seemed long, it was barely five minutes when the scout-master himself appeared in view, with Murphy, at the bend of the road below, and scarcely two hundred yards away.

At sight of them, Danby's heart gave a great leap for joy, and he extended his hand three times, giving the pre-arranged signal, should the enemy be sighted and special assistance needed.

" Had they seen the signal ? " John Holland was sweeping the landscape with his glasses. Now he was turning in Danby's direction, and the signals were immediately repeated.

Yes, thank God! the signals had been observed and understood, for the chief himself had acknowledged them. Danby saw Murphy immediately disappear along the roadway, as though for extra assistance, while the scout-master came up quickly but quietly from cover to cover. He was only fifty yards away now, and Danby gave the signal for extreme caution. In another thirty seconds he was by Danby's side, and a few hurried whispers told all that the chief needed to know.

Twice John Holland himself crept to Danby's original post and watched the men. Yes, there could be no doubt about it. A bundle of documents lay beside them, and one held a chart in his hand. They were talking German, too; making plans for some great coup, and part of the conversation reached the ears of the scout-master. When the chief retired again, he placed his hand on Danby's shoulder, and whispered :—

" Danby, you have made a great find ! If we can capture them both, to-morrow you will be the most famous scout in England. You will deserve a commission in the British Army."

" They're both armed, I am afraid," said the youth. " They may easily get away even yet."

" No, they won't ! " replied Holland, producing for the first time, much to Danby's surprise, a six-chambered revolver, which the magistrate had secretly begged him to take that morning for fear that some of the lads' lives might be endangered during the search.

Danby opened his eyes wide with surprise when he saw the weapon, and that moment he knew that the spies had little chance of escape, for Holland could draw a bead on a sparrow at forty yards. It was the scout-master's intention, however, to take the men alive, if possible, and only to shoot in the last resort. He still waited patiently, therefore, and in another few minutes was rewarded by seeing the other scouts approaching. They had been rounded up smartly by Murphy, who now left them again in response to another hand-signal from the chief.

By another signal, the other three scouts were ordered to make a wide detour and to come up on the other side of the gully ; there to take cover until called.

All was ready now, and Holland did not intend to wait for further assistance. If it came, well and good, if not, then he felt sure the six of them were sufficient to deal with the Germans.

" I will just take one more look over the ridge, Danby, and then we must act. The others will now be in position. But nearly everything will depend on you and myself. Are you ready ? "

"Yes, sir," replied the youth, though there was just a nervous tremor in his voice, but John Holland looked into his eyes and knew he could trust him. The nervousness would pass when the time for action commenced.

"If they refuse to obey my orders, I shall shoot ! "

The next moment they leapt forward to the summit of the little hillock, and Holland, pointing his pistol, shouted :—

"Hands up, or I fire ! "

CHAPTER VIII.

"MAXWELL'S EAGLES."

WITH one bound the Germans sprang to their feet, amazed at the sudden turn of events. The pedlar held up his hands, for he was covered, but the other made a movement towards his side-pocket. The next instant, before he could withdraw his pistol—

"Flash—Bang!" came the report of Holland's weapon, and the man fell to the ground.

At the same instant, Danby gave the scream of an eagle, that could be heard a mile away, and, bounding forward, closed with the pedlar, who, seeing himself uncovered for an instant, had withdrawn his hands and was also drawing his weapon.

"No, you shan't!" cried Danby fiercely, as he grappled with the man, and the two spun round and round, down the gully, rolling over the prickly weeds, stinging nettles, and tufted grass.

Holland stayed only an instant to disarm the wounded German, who was still trying to reach his weapon, and then dashed forward to Danby's assistance.

Meanwhile, the scream of an eagle was repeated from three different throats, as the others closed in to the assistance of Holland and Danby. And in less than five minutes the fight was over. The pedlar was bound with the strong cord of Bancroft's lasso, and the other accomplice, who had only been shot in the leg, was bandaged and treated with every consideration, being placed upon a stretcher which the scouts soon rigged up.

Then it was that the strangest thing of all happened. Shouts and cries were heard mingled with the thud, thud of horses' hoofs rapidly approaching up the other side of the slope. What could it be? Were there more accomplices about the place, and were they coming to the rescue of the spies? The matter was soon settled, when, a moment later, half a dozen horsemen, lancers in British uniforms, appeared on the crest of the hillock, then, deploying and galloping down the gully, they surrounded the scouts and their prisoners.

Following them came three or four officers
of high rank, for they wore the red tabbs of
staff officers. It was General Maxwell with
his staff and escort of lancers. Murphy, when
he returned the second time, met them on the
road, and, stopping them, told them how
matters stood.

The General had smiled pleasantly at the
excited youth, and was about to pass on, when
the report of Holland's weapon, and the shouts
and cries that followed, quickly caused him to
change his mind. Perhaps there was something in the lad's story after all . . . German
spy indeed ? It would be just as well to see.
Then, turning in his saddle, he cried to his
men :—

" Squadron—into line ! Forward—Trot—
Gallop ! " and away they went, the whole body
of officers and men, and mounting the hillock,
they saw for themselves what has just been
described.

Without a moment's delay the prisoners
were searched and examined. Incriminating
letters, documents, plans and secret codes were
found upon them.

" Remove the prisoners, Douglas ! " ordered

the General, to one of his assistants. "Take them to head-quarters!"

"Yes, sir," and in a trice the spies were taken away by several men of the escort.

Then there was a whispered conversation between the General and several members of his staff, which lasted for a couple of minutes, during which such words as these reached the ears of the patrol, who now stood stiffly at attention in the presence of the General :—

"Yes, sir. He is the very same man. We've been after him for weeks. Here is his photograph. He is the brain of the German secret service in this part of England," etc., etc.

"All right, captain. At any rate, it's a deucedly clever haul. He'll get his deserts shortly."

Then turning to the scout-master, the General said :—

"What is your name?"

"John Holland, sir," replied the master.

"And who are these lads?"

"The Eagle Patrol, sir, from the Old Grammar School, Cockfosters, near London, where I am one of the junior masters."

"What are you doing on the East Coast during war time?"

"We are camping down here, during the holidays.   We came down before the outbreak of war."

"I understand that you have caught these men entirely on your own initiative, scout-master?"

"Yes, sir."

"Then let me tell you that you have made a great capture, for you have laid the cleverest spy in England by the heels.   You deserve to be decorated, and these lads rewarded, and by heaven, you shall be!"

"General," said John Holland, saluting and pointing to Danby, "this is the scout who made the discovery.   Let the reward be given to him."

"Tut! tut!   You have all helped, and you seem to have organized the search.   Is there any favour I can grant you?"

"Yes, sir.   There is only one thing we de-sire," replied the scout-master smartly.

"Name it, and if it is in my power to grant it, it shall be yours," said General Maxwell.

"Attach my patrol to your division, General,

and let us serve with you during the war, in England or abroad."

"Do you mean it?"

"Yes, sir."

"Then, if my powers permit it, even by a little stretching, it shall be done. I will communicate with the War Office, and tell them of the service you have rendered to the country, which is considerable, and if permission is given, then yours shall be the first patrol of Boy Scouts to be attached to the British Army. And if I am sent to France with my division, then you shall go with me."

"Thank you, sir, a thousand times!"

"It will be necessary for you to get the consent of these boys' parents, as they are under age, but I don't think there will be any difficulty in doing that. Secure this, and then report yourself to my head-quarters with your patrol in three days from now," said the General, and with that he rode off, with his escort, receiving as he did so the parting salute of the patrol and a wild volley of cheers from the excited and enthusiastic lads.

Oh, the wild delight of the Eagles when they heard this good news from the lips of the

General himself! It cannot be described; it must therefore be left to the imagination. They marched back to camp with light hearts and never once thought of the fatigue. Round the camp fire they shouted and sang till they were hoarse. After dinner, they mounted their bicycles and rode off to the nearest post-office to wire home for the necessary consent. Then, lest their request should be unheeded, they wrote long letters to parents and guardians, telling what had occurred, and begging that the necessary consent might not be delayed.

Danby and Bancroft received replies within three hours, to this effect: "Certainly, by all means." All the rest received them by first post in the morning, save Shackleton, who, after the post arrived, sat about the fire, a picture of misery, for there was no letter for him.

"Cheer up, my boy!" the scout-master said to him. "I don't think the reply will be long now. And when it comes, it's sure to be all right."

"Thank you, sir," the lad would reply. Then he would try to cheer up a little, but, as the hours crept on towards noon, and no answer came to his wire, he felt almost ready to cry. And no wonder, for he saw visions of the other lads marching off to war, and winning glory and honour, but saw himself back at the school-desk.

As they sat down for the midday meal, however, and passed round the smoking soup-kettle, a telegraph boy dashed up the rough track that led to the camp, and cried out :—

"Telegram for Shackleton,
  Eagle Patrol Camp,
    Overstrand,
      Cromer, Norfolk."

"Here!" shouted the excited Shackleton, springing to his feet. Seizing the pink envelope he tore it open, and read aloud for all to hear :—

"Congratulations! The London papers this morning are full of your adventures. Certainly, I give my consent. Am proud of you.
    "JOHN SHACKLETON."

Shackleton felt in his pocket. Yes, he had only one coin left. It was a half-crown. He took it out and gave it to the waiting messenger who had brought him such good tidings. After that, he was as cheerful and bright as the rest of them. His great trial had passed.

Next morning, after a summary trial, Carl Schmidt, alias Pete Donkin, pedlar, alias James Wainwright, ice-cream vendor, and a good many other professions, was shot at daybreak in the Tower of London. He was the first spy to be shot in England for a hundred years, and people about Billingsgate and St. Katherine's looked up, startled, when they heard the sound of a volley, and saw a thin column of smoke arising from the grey walls of the old Tower.

People who claimed to know said that, with him, plans of an invasion of the East Coast of England were also captured, and many other things which were never let out, but all of which went to prove that he was a master-spy who had been weaving his meshes for many years past.

They also said that the Eagle Patrol deserved the highest credit and reward that could be bestowed upon them, and not a few ventured to predict that before the war was over more would be heard about the Eagles.

On the third morning after the capture of the spy, John Holland led his patrol into the presence of General Maxwell. There they stood in line, Willoughby amongst them with bandaged arm and pale face, but with eager, shining eyes. The great soldier, whose breast was covered with several rows of ribbons, shook hands with each lad separately, conversed with them, and listened to their story. Willoughby he patted affectionately on the shoulder, saying :—

" I think you have the honour to be the first Englishman to be wounded by the enemy. I trust you may soon recover and render further service to your king and country," and the blushing lad replied faintly :—

" Thank you, General ! "

Then, General Maxwell, stepping back a few paces, took from his aide-de-camp a message which had just been received from King George, and read as follows :—

" His Majesty desires to congratulate the lads of the Eagle Patrol, now camped at Overstrand, for their brilliant achievement, and their courage and skill, in the capture of a most dangerous enemy."

"Three cheers for His Majesty, King George!" cried John Holland, and the cheers were given vociferously by the scouts. Then the General continued :—

"I have also received permission from the War Office, as a recognition of the brilliant services you have already rendered, to attach your patrol to my own division. From now, you may consider yourself under military command, and rations and pay will be made to you accordingly. Your leader will be gazetted to my staff as a second-lieutenant, and you will still remain under his personal supervision, and as far as possible you will serve together throughout the campaign."

Another burst of cheering came from the lads. Their wildest hopes had been fulfilled to the uttermost. From that date they took up their position at the General's headquarters, and ever afterwards they were known as

MAXWELL'S EAGLES.

CHAPTER IX.

THE EAGLES IN FRANCE.

It was a bright sunny morning in the latter part of August, 1914, when the "Bullfinch," H.M. transport, weighed anchor, and, along with twenty other transports, steamed down Southampton Water. Belgium, with her ruined towns and blazing villages, her people smitten and wasted by the ruthless hand of the invader, had called loudly to Britain ; and this was Britain's answer. It was not sufficient that England, athwart the Gateway of the Seas, should close the German ports, and sweep her commerce from the oceans. She was now sending to France and Belgium a British Army to fight shoulder to shoulder with the *poilus* and *les braves Belges*.

On the "Bullfinch" was part of Maxwell's division, and amongst them were Maxwell's Eagles. As the vessels weighed and steamed in line ahead, cheer after cheer came from the

(94)

shores of the Sound, and were as eagerly returned by the departing soldiers.

As they left Egypt Point and Norris Castle
on their starboard quarter, and entered Stokes
Bay, the warships there manned ship, and
flung to the breeze a stretch of myriad-coloured
flags. Then, as they opened out Portsmouth
Harbour, the saluting battery and the old
"Victory" fired a salute to these first heroes of
the British Expeditionary Force, who were
going to fight for little Belgium, ravished and
despoiled.

With wide-open eyes, the Eagles clustered
about the fore-chains of the "Bullfinch," for
there was little other space; the upper decks
being filled with men, guns, pontoons, and half
a hundred other things that go to make up the
equipment of an army corps. Never before
had the Eagles felt what sea-power meant.
Here was the first army, in a long line of ships
going across the seas, so far without a single
escort.

"Where is the great German Navy of which
we have heard so much?" asked Danby of
John Holland.

The scout-master smiled, as he replied :—

"Their battle-fleets are already bottled up in Wilhelmshaven and the Elbe. Only a few raiders and submarines are now on the seas."

"But shall we have no escort, as we cross the Channel?" asked the youth, not that he feared what the Germans might do, but because he wondered all the more that the Germans who had done so much on the Continent should not make a serious attempt to stop the transport of the British troops.

"Yes, look there!" replied the chief, pointing as he spoke to where seven or eight ugly, vicious-looking craft lay to, under a thin line of smoke, just abreast of the Nab Light.

"Destroyers!" exclaimed several of the scouts at once as they recognized the rakish, waspish craft they had so often observed patrolling the East Coast.

"Yes, destroyers," replied John Holland. "Just watch how they will waltz round us during our trip to France."

Even as he spoke, a couple of flags went up to the mast-head of the parent ship, which was a light cruiser.

"That means full-speed, and double-line ahead, and is addressed to the captains of the transports, who are all Naval Reserve officers. You see, though the main German fleets are closed up within their harbours, there are sure to be a few submarines who have ventured out through the mine-beds, and will probably try to dispute our passage, but it's precious little they will be able to do. A submarine may be top-dog when it is dealing with an unarmed merchant ship, but when it is up against a four-inch gun, and the powerful ram of a thirty-knot destroyer, its position is not to be envied."

" I hope we shall see at least one periscope before we are across, sir," ventured Willoughby, who was now quite convalescent from his wound.

" Perhaps you may, Willoughby. Keep your eyes well-skinned, and you may be rewarded by a sight of one, but it won't be there long," replied the scout-master.

All went well until they were more than half-way across. The men on deck, though packed like herrings, were as merry as sand-boys. To them it was just a great adventure they were going to—to many of them, alas, it meant the last adventure.

7

The British soldier is a great " sport," and
when he has fought with a man he is willing
to be friends again.   He seldom holds malice
long, especially when his enemy has fought
fair and square.   But, on the German side,
there was going to be precious little that could
be called sportsmanship.   It has been placed
on record by an officer who fought through the
retreat from Mons and back again when the
Germans were driven from the Marne, in the
early weeks of the campaign, that when the
British soldiers drove the enemy out of the
villages which they had temporarily occupied,
they became changed men.   This officer
said :—

" When our men followed up the retreating
Germans from the Marne to the Aisne, and on
to Ypres and Dixmude, when they saw the
fair country-side ruined and laid waste,
little farms and cottages wantonly pillaged,
then set on fire, often over the heads of aged
and bed-ridden occupants, when they saw the
stream of homeless peasants and refugees, and
heard their tales of violence, pillage and death,
then the British soldier for the first time
began to ' see red.'   This was no ordinary foe

he was up against, but an unscrupulous and ruthless one. Then it was that those soldiers of the first army, naturally humane, even to tenderness, became terrible in their wrath, and performed deeds of valour which, were they not proved to be authentic, we should have regarded more as fiction than fact."

That is the testimony of a British officer who witnessed these things, and has left them on record.

It must have been a wonderful sight, during that cloudless day in August, when the British transports went across. The "Bullfinch" was the second ship on the starboard line, and therefore, from her fore-chains, where the Eagles were clustered, it was possible to get a good view ahead. The sea was pretty flat, so that it was fairly easy to spot a periscope within a radius of a mile, especially from the bridge, where the look-out and the signallers were constantly on the alert, with their glasses.

Danby was watching a destroyer bringing in a huge German sailing barque. She was a prize ship and was being brought into Dover. The whole line of crowded transports broke into cheering as they saw the white ensign

over the German flag at the mast-head, and
the light cruiser made several contortions with
her semaphore, as she sent her congratulations.

Suddenly, and without the slightest previous
warning, a shot was heard from the cruiser,
and, looking in that direction, Danby saw a
signal flying from her lines.

"What can be the matter?" he wondered.
But the signal which had been flung out
was a very familiar one in the navy, and
meant—

"Scatter submarines."

In a few seconds a couple of the escorting
destroyers dashed ahead, one on either beam
of the cruiser, as though they were making for
some invisible foe. At the same time they
were firing their bow-chasers with wonderful
rapidity. Then the other destroyers waltzed
around the transports as though they were
doing some old-time fairy dance. In fact,
they were covering the transports in such a
way, that no torpedo could reach them, and at
the same time making it impossible for another
submarine to show its periscope.

While all this was going on, the navigating

officers of the transports were using their
helms to the utmost, sending them hard-a-port,
then hard-a-starboard, so that the ships zig-
zagged and rocked like cradles on the surface
of the water. This was done so that, should
the enemy even get a chance to fire a torpedo,
the odds would be greatly against him hitting
the target.

There was tense excitement for a few
minutes. Evidently a German submarine had
crept through the mine-bed between Dover
and Ostend, and meant business. But its
effort was short-lived. The first destroyer
that got off went like a rocket through the
water. Except her ugly black funnels and a
column of smoke nothing could be seen of her,
for a wall of water and white foam stood like
a ridge on either beam.

Her commander had spotted the enemy's
periscope, which lay right ahead, at the same
moment that the cruiser had signalled the
alarm. Away she went, like a hound unleashed, spitting fire from her bow the while.
A streak of white foam coming towards her
showed the trail of the torpedo from the submarine. The destroyer went hard-a-port and

the deadly thing missed her by a few feet. It was the last torpedo she was ever to fire. Before she could submerge into safety, the destroyer was upon her. There was a rasping, grating sound, and the ram of the destroyer, tearing off one side of her conning-tower, passed right over her, and the U-boat went down into the depths.

As the "Bullfinch" passed the spot, the Eagles noticed that the surface of the water was covered by a thick layer of oil, while air bubbles were constantly coming up from below. But there was no sign of wreckage or drowning sailors, for the crew of the U22 had all gone down to their last resting-place on the bed of the ocean.

The destroyer limped back to her station amid the plaudits of the whole fleet, but it was evident that she was making water. She had almost wrenched off her ram, and had started several plates in her bow, so that it was necessary to close her bulk-heads and to take her in tow.

Shortly after this, the French coast appeared in sight, and a French torpedo-boat came out of Boulogne to pilot them into the harbour.

There, the British Army were welcomed with wild enthusiasm by the people, who showered upon them gifts of chocolate and tobacco, and showed them every kindness.

As they marched through the streets and the old city square, shouts of—

"Vive l'Angleterre! Vive le Roi!" greeted their ears.

The heavy cloud which had overshadowed the Land of France for the past fortnight disappeared as if by magic, and the sun shone once again in the land of the olive and the vine.

Not a few traitors, and spies in German pay, had been busy spreading the rumour that Perfidious Albion would never come to the help of Belgium and France, and so for many days anxious eyes had been watching the sea for the coming of the British Army. Now at last it was here.   The English Channel was full of transports and warships, and as the first party came ashore, they received a tremendous greeting.

To the strains of "Bonnie Dundee" the Highlanders, the old allies of France, marched from the quay, while every now and then the excited natives burst forth with the "Hymn of the Republic" :—

> Allons enfants de la Patrie,
> Le jour de gloire est arrivé
> Contre nous de la tyrannie
> L'etendent sanglant est levé.

CHAPTER X.

A BRUSH WITH UHLANS.

THAT night the British Army bivouacked on the heights called Cæsar's Camp, overlooking the city and the English Channel. A hundred and ten years previously Napoleon, with his "Grande Armée," had camped on the same spot, while he waited for his admirals to carry out his orders, which were "to smash Nelson and the British fleet," so that he might carry out his long cherished scheme of invading England. The tidings that he waited for never came, but one day an exhausted courier reached the camp, with the news of the Battle of Trafalgar, the destruction of the French and Spanish fleets, and the capture of Villeneuve, his greatest admiral.

It was with strange feelings that the Eagles lit their fires, and prepared their evening meal. Their thoughts were full of home and loved ones, and every now and then, as the conver-

sation about the camp-fire flagged, they strained
their eyes over the dark, misty seas towards
the England that they loved. But this was
no time for sadness. They were to entrain
early next morning and to be taken straight
to the front, to meet the invaders. So, after
one last look across the sea, they rolled themselves in their blankets, and were soon fast
asleep.

There were no bugles to sound the reveille
next morning, for the only bugle-calls allowed
on active service are the "alarm" and the
"charge." This has been rendered necessary
because, so often in the past, an enemy bugler
or spy has sounded a false alarm, and on one
occasion at least has caused a retreat.

The scout-master, however, who was sleeping near the lads, called them gently at daybreak, saying :—

"Come, boys, the brigades will be falling in
before long. Let us get a good meal as quickly
as we can; we can never be certain of two
meals in the same day now."

Very smartly the lads tumbled out, rolled
up their blankets, and were ready to march before Willoughby, whose turn it was to serve as

orderly, brought their rations from the " cook-house."

Never before has a British Army taken the field so quickly as that which left these shores under Sir John French in August, 1914. On their second day in France they were in touch with the enemy ; on the third day, they were in the thick of the fight. The Eagles were moved up with the first army, and soon got their first taste of real warfare.

It is not the author's intention in this book to give a detailed history of the wonderful deeds of the British Army during this trying campaign ; nor even to show how the two first army corps and a cavalry brigade flung themselves in the path of the victorious Germans, who had trampled Belgium underfoot and were now pressing with forced marches upon Paris. That I must leave to the historian, who will write it later, and who will then tell the world how those two corps, outnumbered five to one, met for a while the whole shock of the Prussian armies, faced the most terrible machine-gun fire the world has ever known, stemmed the rush of the tyrants, and saved Paris.

Rather is it my intention to tell of the simple, brave deeds of the lads of the Eagle Patrol, who but a month previous had been mere schoolboys at the Old Grammar School, and now proved themselves to be heroes.

It was on the evening of their second day in France, when the thin British line had taken up its position on the banks of the canal which runs from Condé on the west, to Mons and Binche on the east, and were rapidly entrenching themselves with picks and shovels, that Danby, who with the other scouts had been busy on various "fatigues," suddenly came across Bancroft holding the horse of an officer, who had just ridden in with dispatches.

"Can you hear that thunder, Banky?" asked Danby. "I fear we're going to have a storm before the night is over."

"Storm?" replied Bancroft in a questioning tone.

"Yes, listen to it! It's thunder in the distance, and it's coming nearer too. There, did you see that flash?"

"It's the sound of the German guns that you hear," said the other in a calm voice, though

Danby noticed that his face seemed just a shade paler.

"Eh, what? The German guns, did you say? Who told you so?" and for once there was a slight tremor in Danby's voice.

"Our Fifth Cavalry Brigade is out yonder under General Chetwode, and they're being driven in, as the Germans are there in great force. Some of them are in a tight corner, I fancy, and I believe this dispatch rider, whose horse I am holding, has brought in serious news. I heard him tell another officer that they're trying to get round our left flank," said Bancroft in a serious tone.

"Phew!" replied his chum. "Then we shall see some real fighting soon."

Danby was right. They would not have long to wait. All that night the roar of the guns increased, and the horizon was red with flashes. Nay, it seemed at times as though the rim of the world was on fire. It was, however, only the burning of the villages and hamlets which marked the approach of the inhuman foe. Sleep was impossible. The soldiers worked all night at preparing the trenches. Each man worked till he was ready to fall with fatigue ; then he laid himself down and slept upon the ground, too tired to eat, and another took his place with the entrenching tools.

" At all costs, boys, these trenches must be finished ! " the officers kept saying to the men. And very often they themselves took off their coats and gave a hand to encourage their men.

Early next morning John Holland called the patrol, and said there was special work to be done. They would be expected to give a hand with the wounded soon, for they were already pouring in, and being carried to the field hospitals behind the lines ; but there was other work to be done which could brook no delay.

" What is it ? " asked the Eagles, for they were anxious to render whatever service they could, though they were a bit tired of camp fatigues, which did not have much spice of danger about them, save perhaps an occasional kick from a vicious horse, or the slight chance of a shock from a live wire which had to be run out and fixed to the entanglements in front of the trenches.

" You see those farm-houses and hamlets out there," said Holland.

" Yes," replied the lads, looking in the di
rection pointed out by their leader.

" Well, there are numbers of them still in-
habited. Some by old folks who refuse to quit
them, for fear their cattle should be stolen
and their crops damaged. The orders are that
they must all be vacated at once ; if necessary,
force must be used in order to save the lives
of these simple people. The houses will soon
be in the direct line of fire, if the enemy continues to advance."

The lads snatched a hasty breakfast, filled
their haversacks with their day's rations, then,
taking a service rifle with ten clips of cartridges
each, away they went on their errand. This
was work they could well do, and as all the
boys spoke a little French, and several of them
spoke it fluently, they were able to point out
to the inhabitants the danger of remaining
where they were. Thus they helped many of
them to carry off their bundles, and assisted
with the infants and the aged. Others were
so obstinate in their resistance that they had
to be removed by force, for they refused to
leave their homes where they had spent all
their days.

Not a few of these latter cases proved to be peasants or small farmers who were in the pay of the Germans, and were thus traitors to their own country. Evidence of this came to hand a little later, and quick justice was meted out to the culprits.

This work was continued well on towards the afternoon, when something happened to interrupt the useful work of the Eagles. The position where this work was being carried out was just a little on the left flank of the British Army, near a wood which stretched down to within a mile and a half of Condé, and which offered some cover to the advancing Germans.

All unknown to the Allies, the Germans were just preparing their outflanking movement, and for a great dash of their Hussar or Uhlan Regiments, round the left flank of the British line.

The Eagles had been removing a very obstinate peasant from his small holding, when Danby noticed a few horsemen issuing from the cover of the wood half a mile away, and called to Holland :—

"Look, sir. What are those horsemen? Are they British cavalry retiring?"

"British cavalry?" cried the leader, shading his eyes with his hand, and looking towards the forest. "They scarcely have the appearance of Britishers."

A moment later he had unstrapped his binoculars, and was keenly scrutinizing the approaching horsemen, about forty in number.

"Good heavens, no! They're Uhlans. Smartly there, Eagles! Take cover under that hedge."

With the precision of well-trained scouts the Eagles took cover under a hedge that lined the road leading from the wood to the little farm.

"Keep steady and cool, lads, and you have nothing to fear," said John Holland, quite calmly. "There are only seven of us, but this hedge is good cover against mounted men. Don't fire till I give the word, and take careful aim; there's nothing to be gained by hurry."

"Never fear, sir, we shall stick it; we're no' afeard o' the brutes," replied MacGregor, tumbling into his native dialect as usual, when something stirred his marrows.

"Another few paces to the left, Murphy. Close up a little, Shackleton. There, that will

8

do. Now keep perfect silence till I give the word," went on the chief in low tones.

Then there followed a couple of minutes of tense silence, during which the Uhlans came up rapidly. The scouts could now hear the thud, thud of the horses' hoofs, the jingle of their accoutrement, and, every now and then, the sound of their voices. On they came, past the bend in the road, the pennons fluttering gaily from their lances, and all the while they were approaching the ambush so neatly laid for them.

All the nervous energy of the Eagles was concentrated on the road along which the enemy must come. It was a period of great tension and strain. At any instant the head of the column might appear and the fight begin.

Not a look was cast behind, which was a pity for once, for, from that quarter, a new danger was threatening.

The whole pathway of the German advance had been carefully prepared, and a network of spies, under every possible guise, made the work of the Allies more and more difficult.

At this very moment, one of these culprits

was signalling to the advancing Germans over
the heads of the scouts who lined the hedge.

The first two Uhlans, thrown out in advance
of the rest as a vedette, were now level with
the scouts. They were supposed to be the
eyes and ears of the squadron, which followed
a little way behind. They looked this way and
that, but, so cleverly had the Eagles taken
cover, that though they searched the hedge
with their eyes, and appeared to be looking
straight at them, yet never a sign did they
make to their companions, to indicate suspicion
or alarm.

The vedette passed, and the main body approached rapidly. They were within forty
paces, when one of them, suddenly pointing
beyond the scouts to the farm, cried out :—

" Ein Rotsignal, mein herr, nicht wahr ? "
which meant, " Is not that a danger-signal. sir ? "

CHAPTER XI

THE ADVANCE GUARD.

JOHN HOLLAND heard the Prussian trooper call to his ober-lieutenant, and he understood the significance of the message.

"Ein Rotsignal, indeed?" he muttered between his teeth. "Who was this traitor signalling from behind their backs to the Uhlans?"

The whole scheme of the ambush was in danger. Casting a hasty glance over his shoulder, the scout-master saw the supposedly aged and infirm peasant whom they had just been assisting. He told them he had been bed-ridden for two years, and, protesting against removal, had complained bitterly of severe pain as the scouts carried him out. Now he was standing erect in the field near the farm, a hundred yards away, and signalling to the approaching Germans with all the vigour of a lusty youth.

"The devil is in German pay!" gasped

Holland. Then, seeing that the Uhlans were
not twenty yards away, he shouted :—

"Fire !" then, "Rapid fire !" but, swerving
round, with his first shot he laid the traitor
behind him dead, before he could finish his
message.

A spurt of flame went out from the hedge,
as the rifles crackled simultaneously. So careful and deliberate had been the first volley
that the lieutenant, the sergeant, and four
troopers rolled from their horses, dead or
wounded. Then followed a scene of wild horror
and consternation. The Uhlans, despite their
advanced guard, had been completely taken by
surprise. The loss of their leaders and the
stampede of riderless horses which ensued did
not help them at all, but increased the confusion.

"An ambush ! Wo ist der hinterhalt ?"
came shouts and cries, mingled with curses and
groans.

"Charge the English swine !" cried some one,
and some of the Uhlans spurred their horses
forward over the prostrate bodies of their
fallen comrades, and tried to force a way
through the tangled growth.

It was useless, for a slimy ditch three feet deep added to the difficulty, and the continued rapid fire of the Eagles was proving most deadly and effective.

Already the roadway was littered with dead and wounded men and struggling horses. It was impossible to miss the target at such close range. Some of the Uhlans, however, had dismounted, and were returning the fire, and the bullets were pinging their way through the hedge about the scouts.

"Steady, Eagles!" John Holland commanded, in calm, unflurried tones, which did much to reassure the lads who were now under fire for the first time.

"Keep well under cover and don't expose yourself. They can't last much longer," and so the fight continued for a few minutes, until the Uhlans, reduced to a third of their original strength, made a dash for their horses, mounted, and galloped away in the direction of the wood. As they did so, the Eagles gave them one parting volley, and then, emerging from their cover, gave a frenzied cheer.

"Well done, Eagles!" cried John Holland. "After this, I can trust you anywhere."

"Anybody hurt?" asked Danby, mustering the patrol, and numbering them.

"All here except Shackleton and Murphy. Where are they?"

"Murphy! Shackleton!" called several voices.

"Here!" came the reply from behind the hedge.

"All safe?" shouted back the patrol-leader.

"Yes, sir, all safe, except Shackleton; he's got a German souvenir, and I'm rendering first aid."

"Nothing serious, I hope?" asked Holland, who was quickly by the lad's side.

"Only a scratch, sir," replied Shackleton, who still lay upon the ground, and spoke bravely but feebly.

John Holland carefully examined the wound, extracted a dark piece of metal from the lad's arm with his forceps; then bandaged the arm and made a sling, exclaiming:—

"It was more than a scratch, Shackleton. It was a fragment of an explosive bullet, I fear. The rascals! But it's missed the bone, and as it's bled freely, I think it'll soon be better; but you must go to the field hospital as soon as you've had a rest."

All the others were safe and sound, though very grimy and mud-spattered. It was a wonder that any of them came out unscathed, however, and it was only owing to the excellent way in which they took cover and kept it. Not a single Uhlan ever caught sight of them during the whole of the fight, and Shackleton's wound came from a chance bullet, as the Germans fired at the flashes. This was proved by the surprise which the wounded Germans showed, when the scouts came out of their cover, and asked them to surrender.

"Gott in Himmel!" exclaimed the wounded sergeant, as John Holland removed his weapons smartly, and then offered to examine his wounds. "Have we been fighting boy scouts?"

"A few of them," replied the scout-master, as he told off the others to attend the wounded, after having disarmed them all.

"Donner und blitz! If your boy scouts fight like this, what will not your army do?"

It was while they were engaged upon this errand of mercy, removing the dead, and attending to the wounded, that Danby, who was giving to a dying trooper with fair hair and blue eyes a drink from his water-bottle, heard once more the clatter of hoofs.

"They're coming on again, sir!" he shouted.

"Who are coming?" asked the chief.

"The Uhlans are coming!"

Dropping the white bandages which he held in his hand, Holland strained his eyes in the direction of the sound.

"Sapristi!" he exclaimed; "they've brought up reinforcements."

Yes, there could be no mistake about it. There, less than half a mile away, was a whole cloud of skirmishers coming up, and after them, squadron after squadron of Uhlans and Prussian Cavalry of the Guard were already debouching from the wood. It was the beginning of the great dash, which nearly succeeded.

The Germans, remembering the success of their Uhlans during the Franco-Prussian War, were attempting a great Hussar ride round the left flank of their opponents. Their orders had been to ride round the flank, cut the British communications, harry the villages, terrorize the populace, next, to roll up the thinly extended British lines, and shut them up within Mauberge, the French frontier fortress. These five squadrons of picked horsemen now approaching were the vanguard of the great offensive.

There was not an instant to be lost, and John Holland ordered the Eagles back to cover, for he knew already from what had occurred at fifty places in Belgium that scant mercy could be expected from the enemy, even if the lads continued their attention to the wounded.

While the Eagles doubled back towards the English lines, under cover of hedges, trees, orchards, and small plantations, they heard the constant whir-r-r of the aeroplanes overhead. Some of these were French and British, scouting for movements of the enemy.

" I wonder if our men have seen them, sir ? " asked Danby of the scout-master, as soon as they had proceeded a little way.

" Yes, our air scouts are sure to have reported the fight with the Uhlans," he replied. " I saw at least two of our own aeroplanes overhead while we were engaged in the scrap."

"I wish we could signal back information to head-quarters," said the youth in an anxious tone. "If they're not discovered in time, it may be too late."

"Never fear! Our people are not asleep. Listen to that."

At that moment something very much like a British cheer was borne upon the breeze, and, straining his eyes, Danby saw a cloud of dust, and heard quite distinctly the clatter of hoofs coming towards him from the direction of the English lines.

"British cavalry!" cried Bancroft, tumbling to a solution at once.

"I hope it is, or else we're surrounded and done for," cried another of the lads.

"Yes, British cavalry without a doubt!" cried the scout-master, looking through his binoculars. "I can make out three squadrons, Scots Greys, Lancers and Hussars; part of Chetwode's Brigade, I believe. Hurry up, Eagles, there's going to be a cavalry charge."

"Hurrah!" shouted the excited youths, carried away for a moment by a wave of enthusiasm, as they saw the squadrons coming up at the trot.

"It's going to be another 'Balaclava Charge,' lads. We're in luck's way this time. We shall see it all from this mound," cried Murphy.

At this, the Eagles raced for a slight elevation of ground, near a copse, which overlooked the probable site of the coming fight.

On came the Prussians, five full squadrons, towards the bend in the road, where the track widened into a little green about half an acre in extent, and where a shrine of the Madonna and Infant had been erected by the pious villagers who dwelt hereabouts. Neither column had as yet seen their opponents, but the bend in the road would shortly reveal them to each other, even if their vedettes did not raise the alarm.

"Look! They have caught sight of each other," cried Danby. "Now for it!"

It was but a small affair after all, taken into consideration with the huge armies that were now preparing to face each other elsewhere, but it had this significance: it was the first time that British and German cavalry encountered each other.

Immediately the columns became aware of

each other's presence, orders were given on both sides to reach the open space quickly so as to enable the squadrons to deploy. And at the word "Gallop!" a race commenced for the point of vantage.

CHAPTER XII.

A SKIRMISH.

ALMOST together the opposing forces entered the arena, which was far too confined, so that some of the men had to leap the ditch and hedge to get into touch, but for the most part the fight took place on the green.

"Squadron into line! Left wheel!" cried the British commander. Then almost immediately after :—

"Char-r-ge!"

The orders came simultaneously from both sides, as into that narrow, confined space the finest horsemen of two great empires dashed with tremendous impact. An eyewitness has said that the shock of their meeting was like thunder, and that the ground trembled with the tramp, tramp of the horses, while the air resounded with the shouts of men, the blast of trumpets, and the clash of steel. It was like one of the Homeric contests, for the men fought hand to hand. Troopers and horses were mixed up in an inextricable, seething, struggling, writhing mass.

The Prussians were big men, mounted on heavy horses, and when they began the charge they went full pelt, but ere the shock, many of them seemed to lose heart and slacken off almost unconsciously, as though they had no relish for cold steel. Yet the enemy had the advantage of numbers, and were at least five to three. But the superiority of the British, despite these disadvantages, was immediately evident. At the first charge our men rode through them like blotting-paper, then, wheeling round, fought them sword to sword, and saddle to saddle. As the other squadrons came up, this process was repeated time after time, until, discomfited and beaten, the remnant of the enemy fled from the spot, pursued by our men for more than a mile.

Thus ended one of the first brilliant episodes at the opening of the war. It was the beginning and the end of cavalry work, for very soon after, the line of battle, from the Swiss Alps to the North Sea, was a series of trenches and barbed wire entanglements, which made cavalry charges impossible.

As the Eagles returned to the rear of the British lines that afternoon, tired out with the exertions and the excitement of the day, the thunder of artillery, which had long been heard in the distance, grew fiercer and fiercer. It was one of the most critical days in the history of the British Army. Shells were already bursting over the outskirts of Mons. Four German corps, with over six hundred guns, and several divisions of cavalry, were marching through Ath and the Forest of Soignies, upon the thin line of khaki which held the English front.

There was to be no sleep that night, for, as evening drew on, every fighting man was required in the trenches to repel the enemy's attacks, and for non-combatants there were hundreds of fatigues to be performed.

No sooner had the Eagles passed their wounded comrade to the Field Ambulance, than a staff officer riding by espied Holland, and after a brief sentence or two, ordered him to take his patrol and assist in carrying in the wounded.

As the major rode off, Holland returned to the boys, and ordered :—

"Eagles, fall in! About turn! Quick march!"

Then they started off for the trenches to give a hand with the stretchers. The sight that met their eyes when they reached the second trench was dreadful. The enemy's shrapnel had already made great gaps in the lines, and the din and noise was horrible. But the worst was yet to come.

A battery of quick-firing guns was stationed close to where the Eagles were working. They were belching forth a leaden hail over the heads of the men in the front trenches, but so well were they screened by brushwood and trees, that up till now the enemy had failed to locate them.

Suddenly, out of the gloom of the forest a little way ahead three aeroplanes shot forth like sparrow-hawks. Over the British lines they flew, circling and swooping about till they were right overhead.

"Look out! There's a bomb!" cried Bancroft as they watched a trail of smoke descending from the first Taube.

The next minute, all the guns of that battery were pointed up at the intruders, while the officer in charge kept constantly calling out the ranges.

"Two thousand—two thousand five hundred!" then "Left, one degree—one and a half!"

"Got it! Hurrah!" and a cheer went up as the nearest enemy plane turned a complete somersault in mid-air and came down with its petrol tank all ablaze.

"Bravo, Gunner Langford!" shouted the battery officer. "You're the first man to bring down a German aeroplane!"

Then the cheering was taken up all along the front line trench, for the incident was so thrilling that the men had been watching it with keen interest.

"That was a direct hit, gunner! Now try the others!" but there was no need to carry out this part of the officer's command, for at that instant :—

"Whir-r-r, pop-pop, whir-r-r!" was heard in the rear of the lines, and two British aeroplanes, soaring up into the sky, closed with the intruders, and after a sharp fight with machine-guns, drove them off discomfited.

The wrecked Taube had done its work, however, for the black column of smoke which descended was no bomb, but a cunningly devised stratagem for spotting the battery, and thus communicating its exact position to the enemy. This became only too evident when, thirty seconds later, half a dozen high-explosive shells fell all about the gunners, wrecking completely two of the guns, and killing and wounding half the men who still stayed to serve them.

Once again the Eagles were ordered to cover; this time into a trench dug-out, which was being prepared for the second line.

Then it was, late in the afternoon, that the Germans made their greatest efforts at Mons. Their artillery had been preparing the way for hours, and now the fiat had gone forth to advance, and to wipe the British Army off the face of the earth. Some said that the Kaiser himself was behind those blue-grey lines of advancing Prussians, and had addressed the regiments of the famous Prussian Guard, and had told them it was his royal will and order that they should advance and walk over Sir John French's contemptible little army.

Whether this was true or not, the Prussian Generals, Von Buelow and Von Kluck, evidently thought that with five to one they would easily hurl the British from their position.

As soon as it became impossible to carry the wounded through the fire zone, the Eagles managed to take their rifles and get alongside one of the West Yorkshire Regiments in Cuthbert's Brigade, in the front trench, close by the canal.

Then came the moment of the massed attack. The thunder of the guns ceased as if by magic, and the silence that followed became even more oppressive than when they were firing.

" Look out, West Riding, the Bosches are a-cumin'! " cried a sturdy tike fra' Wakefield.

" Look at 'em, lads ! They're cumin' up i' bunches. It's like Cup Day at Sheffield. We can't miss 'em ! "

" Silence, boys ! Get ready, but don't fire yet ! " cried the major of the company.

Then there was another silence, save for the voice of the range-finder, speaking deliberately :—

"Eight hundred yards, seven-fifty, seven hundred! Wait till five hundred, boys, and then give it 'em!"

Danby was just longing to unloose his rifle, but restrained himself. He could now see distinctly the surging crowd of Germans coming on in close formation. He could hear snatches of their singing :—

"Die Wacht am Rhein!" and "Deutschland, Deutschland über alles!"

"Five hundred and fifty, five hundred!" called the range-finder. Then a sharp voice rang out :—

"Fire!"

Suddenly a spurt of flame burst from the British trenches. A hurricane of fire, in which rifles, maxims, and batteries of quick-firers joined, ploughed and shattered the first wave of on-coming Germans. Like drunken men they staggered and reeled, then fell to rise no more. Not a man reached the British trench, or even the bank of the canal.

The Germans had believed that their artillery had beaten down the English defence, and smashed their trenches, so that nothing remained but to take possession of the same.

The lull in the firing which had preceded the attack had doubly convinced them that this was so. Thousands of German dead and wounded covered the field. In some places the dead were piled in ranks, behind which the remnant who remained sheltered.

The German marshals, however, had the advantage of numbers. Never a moment's rest was allowed. Fresh formations were rushed up, the artillery began again, and the massed attacks recommenced. Again and again they met with the same fate. The rifles of the British in the front trenches became so hot with the constant firing that it was almost impossible to hold them, and fresh rifles had to be brought up.

The first success, despite the numbers of the enemy, remained with the English. If only all the line had been so steadfast, there would have been no retreat from Mons. Imagine, therefore, when evening came and the sky was alight once more with burning villages, star-shells and bursting shrapnel, the intense surprise of the British wnen they received the order to retreat.

"Retreat be hanged!" said one of the Yorkshires to his chum. "We've beaten 'em, Bill. Beaten the blighters fair an' square, an' we'll beat the devils agen."

"B Company, fall in there smartly!" called a young lieutenant. "The Brigade will take up a new position in the rear!"

Some say that not a few of the Yorkshires absolutely refused to retreat, until threatened with death for insubordination.

"Why should we retreat?" said one man to his officer. "We've gi'en 'em socks, an' we'll gie 'em hell to-morn!"

In some cases the officers had to plead with the men to get them to fall in with the retreating column. Even then, some begged permission to stay with the guns, which were to cover the retreat. Some little bands of desperate men even broke away, and stayed to fight the advancing Germans on the morrow, and were all killed or taken prisoners. But it had to be. Somewhere to the right of the British line, where the French held the banks of the Sambre and the Meuse, an accident had occurred.

What it was, no one knew as yet. Some said that the French line had cracked under great pressure, and had given way. Others told ugly stories of treason within the French ranks. Certain it was that many German spies were captured behind the lines of the Allies. Signal-posts, telephones, and secret codes, wires and other contrivances had been discovered.

These spies, when caught thus red-handed, met with scant justice. A brick wall, a firing squad, and their fate was sealed. There were hundreds of such enemies, and they were discovered daily.

Thus began the great retreat from Mons, for, the French having gone back on the right wing, it was necessary to keep the line intact, just as Wellington, at Quatre Bras, retreated on Waterloo, because Napoleon had smashed the Prussians on his left wing at Ligny.

CHAPTER XIII.

TAPPING THE ENEMY'S WIRE.

"EAGLES, fall in!" shouted John Holland, just as the first faint tinge of dawn began to show towards the east.

"The Eagles will march with the Ambulance Column of the 13th Brigade, and render all possible assistance during the day."

The lads, thus disturbed from their sound slumbers upon the ground, where they had bivouacked, raised themselves, rubbed their eyes, and fell in. Still only half-awake, they seemed to be conscious of some pending disaster. What were all these columns of horses and men, transport and guns filing past? This was not the same army, surely, with which they had marched against the enemy a few days before!

What could it mean? Were the British Army defeated? Had they been driven from their position ? Surely not ; they would awake soon and continue the march to victory.

For a few moments they stood by and watched the procession, wearied with fighting and trench-digging, and blackened with grime, march past ; then, as the Ambulance Column came along, they received the order :—

"Left wheel. Quick march !" and, taking up their appointed station, marched with the rest, hungry, thirsty, and still aching with fatigue.

As the sun rose, and the grey mists were lifted off the landscape, as if by magic things became more cheerful, and the men began to burst out with

> It's a long, long way to Tipperary,

and snatches of other songs. Then some one would call out :—

"Are we down-hearted ?" and from a thousand throats would come a mighty, reverberating "No-o-o !" followed by bursts of laughter. No, this was not a defeated army. Yesterday, they fought five against twenty, and faced the fire of six hundred guns without flinching. This morning they expected to continue the " sport," but, to their amazement, they had received the order to retreat. It was a very bitter pill, and so for a while they marched breakfastless in the grey light of early dawn. But they soon resumed their usual cheerfulness, and felt that whatever strategy it was that demanded a retreat, it was not because they were beaten. They had still a shot in the locker, and the Prussians would know it in good time.

So the Eagles marched with the rest, from Mons to Landrecies. The wagons and motors of the Ambulance Column were almost filled with wounded men, and as they proceeded, during the intense heat of the morning, many others fell fainting by the roadside. The scouts rendered incalculable assistance to these men, finding water, priceless water for them ; carrying cans of beef-tea from the motor-kitchen, and lifting the men on to the wagons. Thus they saved many precious lives, and the more lightly wounded from falling into the enemies' hands and suffering, perhaps, years of rigorous imprisonment with harsh treatment and insufficient food, in fact, a life of misery.

It was while they were engaged on these errands of mercy, during the midday halt, that the following incident occurred.

The column were resting in the beautiful and picturesque forest of Mormal, and the water supply had entirely failed, so the lads volunteered to take a large soup kettle each and find some well or stream in the neighbourhood. They had proceeded about a quarter of a mile, and had succeeded in finding a woodman's cottage, from whence they secured the water and started to return. As they did so, Bancroft, who was leading, tripped over something, and fell headlong into the bracken and prickly scrub.

"Hurt yourself, old fellow?" cried Danby, who was just behind him.

"No, I think not," replied his chum, jumping up again smartly, and extricating a few thorns from his bare knees.

"Whatever was it you stumbled over?"

"Oh, a tree root, I expect, buried in the bracken there."

At that instant Murphy, coming up a few yards to the left with his kettle, also tripped and went over, exclaiming as he did so :—

"Confound the wire!"

"Wire, did you say?" cried Danby, turning round sharply upon the youth.

"Yes, look, there are miles of it. Poachers, I suppose, after the rabbits."

As he spoke, he lifted up a long line of wire that seemed to run throughout the whole length of the forest.

"Humph!" ejaculated Danby. "Poachers, indeed! I thought you were a first-class scout, Murphy?"

"What else can it be?" replied the scout, looking up at the patrol-leader, and resting his foot on the upturned soup kettle.

"A telephone wire," replied Danby, examining it carefully. "I shouldn't wonder if it were a German wire, laid to some secret outpost in the rear of our lines."

"Golly! A German wire?" exclaimed the rest, who were now clustering round.

"Let's follow it. It should lead us to something," urged Bancroft.

"Let's tap it rather," cried MacGregor, the telephone expert of the patrol, producing a pair of clippers and a neat little box of telephone apparatus.

"Capital idea, MacGregor, that of yours, but even if it isn't coded, the message will be in German, and I doubt whether even Banky there will be able to tackle it, and he's our best German scholar. If we had the chief here now, we could do something. He speaks German like a native."

"So he would!" they all agreed.

"Well now, it's only another four hundred yards back to the column. Just do a sprint, Murphy, will you, as your can's empty, and fetch Mr. Holland. I'll keep the position while you return. The rest of you had better do a double with the soup kettles. The water is wanted urgently for those poor fellows, and we haven't much time to spare, by the growl of those guns, which are getting devilishly close," said Danby. And the next moment they had hurried off, leaving the patrol-leader alone.

In a very short time they were all back again, and with them came the scout-master.

"Snip, snip!" went the cutters, as soon as they had found both the receiving and transmitting wires.

"Quick, Murphy, with that second receiver. Thank you. There now, we're ready.

Hush!" and the chief held up his hand for silence.

Yes, there was no doubt about it, now. It was a cunningly laid German wire. A voice, speaking in plain, uncoded German from somewhere in the neighbourhood, was giving the position, numbers, and direction of Maxwell's division, and requesting that a strong cavalry force be urgently sent through the forest, to fall upon the long column and cut it in halves. Further directions would be sent within half an hour.

"Danby, where are you?" asked the chief, raising his head, as soon as the speaker at the end of the wire had finished.

"Here, sir," answered the patrol-leader, smartly.

"Just take this message back to the column. See that it gets into the hands of some staff officer. It is most urgent. A serious attack on the flank of Maxwell's division is being prepared."

"Yes, sir," replied Danby. Then, saluting he took the brief message which Holland had scribbled out and disappeared into the depth of the forest, which at this spot was very thick.

Meanwhile, Murphy had joined the wires, so that the enemy might not suspect anything.

"Quick, lads!" exclaimed Holland, rising from the ground on which he had been kneeling all this time. "We must find this hornet's nest. I have left the lines intact for a while. Let us follow the wire. This way; the message comes from this end, lads!" and the next moment, keeping good cover, the Eagles started with not a little eagerness, despite their fatigue, to find the end of the thin strand of wire.

Straight through the forest it led them, until they came suddenly upon another tiny woodman's dwelling. Here, a rude fence marked off a small garden, and the wire became one of several strands of ordinary, rusty, barbed wire, running along the fence, in such a way as to arouse the suspicions of no one.

"Deucedly clever, all this!" whispered the scout-master, as he saw how one wire resembled the other.

"Keep your cover, Eagles! I expect we shall find something here," he added, as he stayed a few seconds to scrutinize the building.

"But the wire passes the place, and runs into the forest again, sir," whispered Bancroft.

"Here it is!" said Murphy, who had gone a few yards in advance and picked up the strand again. "It runs behind the fence towards that tree over there."

"Which tree, Murphy?"

"That one with the pigeon-cote fixed up on the branches, sir."

"Ah, so it does. Now their little plot is exposed. It's as simple as can be. Listen to that cooing. There must be fifty birds there, and they're all trained carrier pigeons. Look, there they come in every few minutes; every bird with a message from some accomplice." Then, lifting his forefinger, he whispered :—

"Keep your cover, Eagles, or you're all dead men. There are armed Germans in that cote, and the slightest movement will betray you."

CHAPTER XIV.

THE HORNET'S NEST.

TAKING cover behind the trees and scrub, the Eagles waited a few moments while John Holland brought his glasses to bear upon the little structure, half-hidden amongst the branches.

Yes, there could be no doubt about it. There were at least two Germans there, for he could hear voices. Perhaps they were already 'phoning again ; sending another message to the rapidly advancing German lines. That could be stopped, at any rate. There were only two wires leaving the cote, and they were the ones which had already been tapped. Murphy still held them at a point where they ran through the long undergrowth. At a signal from the chief, he was ready to cut them. All other messages came from the carrier pigeons, which at irregular but brief intervals came sailing over the tree-tops from half a dozen directions, then, spreading their powerful wings, glided down, alighted on the little foot-board and entered the cote. There, the little quills, containing the messages, written on very thin rolled paper, were removed, and the messages decoded, ready for transmitting to headquarters.

"Hist!" Through the little opening where the pigeons entered there came the sound of a gruff voice. Another message was being sent.

"You infernal spies, that shall be your last message!" hissed the scout-master, half-aloud, as he gave a quick signal to Murphy, who held the clippers.

Snip—snip! and the wires were cut.

"Himmel! Donner und blitz!" came several fierce exclamations from the cote, and a voice in German was heard to exclaim, "Fritz, the wires are cut!"

"Destroy the messages quickly, sergeant, before the devils come up. Here, reach me that cipher-code!" said another voice.

"Eagles, present arms!" cried the chief, then, springing from his cover, he called loudly to the spies :—

"Surrender, or you are dead men!"

The answer was a bullet, which carried off the scout-master's hat.

"Fire! Rapid fire!" came the instant command, and for the space of thirty seconds the patrol poured volley after volley into the cote, until it was riddled with holes.

"Cease fire!" shouted Holland, himself advancing at the double till he came quite underneath the structure.

It was time to cease firing, for there was not a square foot of the cote which had not been holed by the bullets. But there seemed no way to enter the structure, save by climbing the tree, for the rope-ladder had been drawn up and the trap-door let down.

"Eagles, advance!" came the order, and the boys came up at the double; their rifles loaded and held at the trail, ready for any emergency.

"They must be all dead, sir," exclaimed Danby, "blown to bits by our fire."

"Yes, I fancy so," replied Holland. "But I should like that cipher-code at once."

"Let me get it, sir!" urged Danby.

"It's a difficult tree to climb. You see, they

have cut away all the lower branches, the artful beggars."

"Give me a lift up on your shoulders, and I'll make a jump for that lowest branch, sir."

"You'll never do it, Danby. We want a rope."

"Bancroft's lasso will do, sir."

"Yes, capital!"

"Bancroft!" called several voices.

"Here, sir," responded that youth, who was already uncoiling his rope. In another ten seconds he had whirled it, so that it not only went over the branch, but the other end came tumbling down at their feet.

"Smart throw, Banky!" cried Danby, as he sprang several feet up the rope, and then shinned up smartly to the lowest bough, followed by MacGregor.

The patrol-leader quickly reached the trap-door, but found it fast. Evidently it was bolted on the inside.

"A hatchet, quickly!" he shouted.

"Here it is," cried MacGregor, catching the handle from Murphy, and passing it up to Danby.

Bang—bang, smash—smash! and the wood

flew in splinters, as the lad blazed away at
the trap-door just above his head.   While this
was going on, there came a cry from one of
the lads :—

"The hut's on fire, sir."

"So it is!" exclaimed John Holland.   "The
rascals have fired it to destroy the codes and
messages."

Smoke was already pouring from the
crevices, and the holes about the foot-boards.
The poor, imprisoned birds were heard fluttering and screeching inside the cote.   Several
other carrier pigeons that glided over the tree-
tops, bringing messages just then, were scared
away by the vaporous fumes, which smelt
strongly of chemicals.

John Holland had one fear.   What if there
were bombs or explosives in the cote.   Instantly the thought crossed his mind; he
thought of the safety of the lads and
shouted :—

"Come down, Danby! MacGregor, come
down quickly!—jump, there may be explosives
in the cote."

But Danby had got through, and did not
hear him.   Only MacGregor jumped in re-

sponse to the chief's orders. The patrol-leader was head and shoulders inside. The next instant, he was hidden from sight.

As he leapt or wriggled through the small aperture he had made, he saw the dead bodies of the two Germans. They had been riddled with bullets. He could see little else, for the place was filled with blinding smoke and red flames. The poor birds were still fluttering about and around. He noticed that the hut itself was not yet in flames, however, but something on the floor was burning.

He picked it up. It was a heap of papers, and records, documents, etc., which had been fired to prevent their falling into the hands of the enemy. It had been the intention of the Germans to blow up the place, when all hope of escape had been cut off, but they were caught so suddenly, when they least expected a surprise, that they had not time to carry out their intention.

Danby quickly seized the flaming material and flung it through the trap-door, where the Eagles below stamped out the blaze, and saved a considerable portion of it. Then he stayed but to open the trap wires, and liberate the birds, for he could not bear to think of their being either suffocated or roasted alive. He had kept pigeons himself, at the old farmstead, and they had been amongst his earliest friends ; for, when a lad of seven, they would come at his call from the roof of the red-tiled barn, and feed from his hands.

This last kindly act nearly cost him his life. Blinded and half-choked by the chemical fumes, he slid down through the trap-door, and dropped senseless into the arms of John Holland, who, foreseeing what would happen, braced himself and caught the lad, breaking his fall. They both rolled to the earth together, for it was a drop of at least eighteen feet, but the scout-master quickly recovering himself, picked up the lad and carried him away, out of danger of any explosion. Then he laid him down in the forest and applied restoratives, until at length Danby opened his eyes again, and asked feebly :—

" Where am I ? "

Then, seeing the lads around him, and hearing the guns booming away in the distance, he smiled weakly, and sat up.

" Bravo, Oscar Danby ! " said John Holland.

"It was the bravest deed I have ever seen, and I shall report it to head-quarters, as soon as I get back."

"It was nothing, sir," replied the lad, modestly. Then, looking towards the tree, he noticed that the cote was still standing intact.

"So it wasn't burnt down after all, sir," he said, pointing towards it.

"No, but it would have been, had you not acted as you did. It was a veritable hornet's nest—one of the head-quarters of the enemy's secret service. I have sent Murphy off to report, and I believe the General will send down a telephone section shortly, and run the place as long as he can as a counter-move, using the carrier pigeons, which you see are still bringing in messages intended for the enemy. I believe the information we have already sent to head-quarters will prove of considerable value, and will enable General Maxwell to counter the enemy's move."

"I am very glad to hear you say that the patrol have already been of some use, sir," replied Danby, making an effort and gaining his feet.

At that instant, the thud of horses' feet was

heard on the soft ground, and almost immediately a bunch of staff officers, belonging to
Maxwell's division, an armed escort of Hussars,
and a telephone section, all mounted, from the
Royal Engineers, came into view.

The patrol formed up and saluted as the
officers came by.

" Are you Maxwell's Eagles ? " cried a major.

" Yes, sir," replied John Holland.

" Then let me inform you that the General
is highly pleased with the service you have
rendered, and when opportunity offers, he
hopes to thank you all personally for the good
work you have done.   The message you tapped
has now been confirmed from other sources,
and dispositions have been made to offer a
counter offensive.   It is just possible that you
may have saved the whole division from a
great disaster."

" Thank you, sir," cried the whole patrol.

" And now which is this other nest you have
found ? "

For answer John Holland pointed to the
pigeon-cote, and the severed wires.

" By Jove, look there, Wilson ! Carrier
pigeons too, droves of them. Just overhaul

these papers, and let me know what they contain.   And I say, Lieutenant?"

"Yes, sir."

"Get your section to work immediately upon those wires. We haven't much time. The First Corps have been hard hit, and are falling back to join the others."

And the engineers went to work at once, while the Eagles, their work done, were ordered by the major to take a bee-line through the forest in another direction, and to rejoin the retreating army. The 13th Brigade had long since gone by, but they might just catch them at their bivouacs that evening if they hurried off in the direction given.

CHAPTER XV.

A DESPERATE RIDE.

As the Eagles made off through the forest of Mormal, hoping to rejoin the 13th Brigade that evening, they could hear the sinister roar of the guns in their rear and on their left flank. The British Army, forced by circumstances beyond its control, was retreating sullenly, from Mons to Landrecies, and from Landrecies to the Marne. And all the time a dogged rearguard action was being fought.

It was indeed a critical time for Sir John French's little army. A rear-guard action is at all times a difficult and dangerous proceeding. But when the retreating force is assailed in its rear and on its flank by overwhelming numbers, then its position is perilous in the extreme. Only the best troops can stand such a hammering without breaking up. When the history of the war is finally written, however, it will probably be said that this brilliant retreat from Mons to the Marne in August, 1914, was the greatest achievement in the whole war.

"Why can't we stand and fight here?" the British soldiers kept asking their officers. "We're more than a match for the lot of 'em. All we ask is to stay where we are and fight them," but the officers could only tighten their lips and reply :—

"Further back yet, lads. The orders are that we must still go back, but our chance will come before long," and many an eyewitness has told how some of these ragged, footsore, and bearded men actually wept, because they were not allowed to make a stand until they came to the banks of the Marne.

So back they went, but every now and then they turned fiercely upon the foe at their heels, as Crawford did with the Light Division when he covered the retreat of Sir John Moore at Corunna. Then, for a few hours, there was a bit of fighting that rejoiced the heart of the weary battalions. Sometimes a brigade of Highlanders, Fusiliers and Guards would get home with the bayonet, or a few squadrons of Dragoons and Lancers with the lance and sword, and then blows were exchanged as in days gone by, but the rifle, machine gun and heavy artillery were generally preferred by Fritz in preference to cold steel. Generally speaking, the British Tommy was a better trained hand-to-hand fighter.

As evening drew on apace, the scouts were compelled to bivouac in the forest, for twice they had missed their way, and had been unable to join their brigade.

"Better stay here, lads, till morning," John Holland had said, for he knew the Eagles were all fagged out with the day's work. Moreover, they had not had a hot meal for two days. Danby, also, on account of his accident, had given out, and must either rest or be carried.

So they lighted their fire, cooked their bully-beef stew, and made hot coffee. Then, putting out the fire lest it should become a mark for some advanced party of Germans, they set a guard, rolled themselves in their blankets, and, despite the wet drizzle which had set in, were soon fast asleep.

Next morning they were up before dawn, for the heavy firing told them that the enemy was advancing more rapidly still. So near were they that at times shells came screaming over the trees, and burst in the forest, sometimes bringing down the trees that barred their way.

Fortunately the night's rest had completely restored Danby, and they started off in the darkness, guided by the scout-master's compass. They did not wait for breakfast, but filling their water-bottles at the little rivulet by which they had bivouacked, they munched their small bread rations on the march.

When dawn came, they had covered a considerable distance, and had edged away a little from the sound of the firing   Then a halt was called, and by the aid of a map Holland tried to locate their exact position, and also to work out the probable position of the 13th Brigade, which they were all anxious to rejoin.

Suddenly, while they were thus resting, a crackle of rifle fire disturbed them in the near distance.

"Listen!" cried the chief, springing to his feet.

Again the sound came, and now they heard also wild shouts, and the sharp clatter of horses' hoofs, coming down a rough track or stony gully, which cut the forest at this point. Instantly, they were all on the alert, and the muzzles of six rifles peeped out from the cover, which they had quickly taken, as if by instinct.

"Eagles, be prepared!" the chief said quietly. "That rifle fire sounds suspiciously German."

"How does the chief know that?" whispered Willoughby to Danby, whose cover he shared.

"It was too mechanical for British fire," replied the other. "Listen to that. British fire is much more independent and irregular. That sounds too much like the drill-book."

"Look! here comes the horseman. He is pursued by some one," exclaimed Danby in low tones.

At that instant a sergeant of the 20th Hussars, well-mounted on a fine bay mare, dashed at full tilt down the gully, then galloped rapidly into view, as he reached the little clearing where the Eagles had taken cover. He was bleeding profusely from a wound in the head, and his tunic was torn in shreds, having been pierced by many bullets.

"A dispatch rider!" cried one of the Eagles.

Immediately afterwards, half a dozen Uhlans, mounted on strapping horses, appeared in pursuit, firing their revolvers at the Englishman.

"Fire!" commanded Holland, and from the unsuspected cover, six rifles spoke out. Three of the Uhlans toppled from their horses. Another swayed in the saddle, but the other two wheeled round and galloped back, after emptying their pistols in the direction of the scouts.

The wounded Hussar, finding himself amongst friends, attempted to rein in his horse, but, even as the mare came to a standstill, the poor fellow, wounded in half a dozen places, fell from the saddle to the earth, and almost fainted from sheer loss of blood.

"Poor fellow!" exclaimed John Holland. "Let me bandage your wounds," and he brought out his pocket-case, which served him for an emergency "first-aid." The sergeant, however, smiled his thanks, but pointed to the dispatch-case, fastened to the saddle.

"Too late," he said, as the scout-master proceeded to examine his wounds. "Too late. Will you deliver those—dispatches—please?"

It was with difficulty that he spoke at all,

for he was so badly wounded in the head and side, and the saddle and stirrups were all covered with his blood.

"To whom must they be delivered?" asked John Holland, bending down and supporting the sergeant in his arms.

"To . . . General . . . Hamilton . . . Third . . . Division," gasped the dying man. Having said this, his eyes closed and his head fell back on to Holland's shoulder. He was dead.

"Eagles," said John Holland, wiping away just a suspicion of a tear from his eye, "you have just witnessed the death of a brave man. He has given his life for his country. He valued those dispatches more than his life. At all costs we must deliver them to General Hamilton."

"We will, sir!" they all cried eagerly, while each one desired the honour for himself. Danby, as patrol-leader, however, claimed the post.

"Yes, I think you had better go, Danby. Are you sure you are quite well, though, after your accident yesterday?"

"Yes, sir, quite well. And if you will let

Willoughby come with me, he can ride the spare horse belonging to the dead Uhlan."

"Very well, Willoughby shall go with you. You must deliver them at the earliest moment to General Hamilton, Commander of the Third Division.   He is with the Second Army Corps, somewhere on the line of retreat.   After you have delivered them, report yourself to the head-quarters of the 13th Brigade."

"Yes, sir.   I shall do my utmost."

The bay mare and the Uhlan's horse were captured, and then the two boys mounted, and, bidding good-bye, galloped off down the road, which at this point crossed the forest.

Meanwhile, the Eagles dragged the body of the dead Hussar into the forest, and, covering it with bracken and leaves, briefly performed the last sad rites over it.   Then they did the same with the bodies of the three Uhlans, for the fourth had escaped with the rest.   They had no time to dig graves, for they expected at any moment that enemy reinforcements might appear.   When they had done all this, they slipped back into the forest, and before nightfall were fortunate enough to rejoin the brigade.

But Danby and Willoughby rode on. Through the greater part of that day they continued their journey, crossing swamps, and swimming rivers where the bridges had been destroyed. Twice they had a slight brush with the enemy's outposts, and once they were pursued by Uhlans, but, as they were well mounted, and both happened to be good horsemen, they got clean away. At length they struck the rear-guard of the Eighth Brigade under Brigadier-General Doran. This was part of the Third Division under Hamilton, and late that afternoon, after their venturesome and somewhat desperate ride, they were escorted to the head-quarters of the General, and personally handed him the dispatch.

It proved to be a very important document, and reported a threatened raid by a highly mobile German column, composed of four cavalry divisions, with batteries of horse artillery, on the British left. The object of the raid was to blow up the bridges, cut the railways, and to sever the communications of the British forces from their bases at Boulogne and Havre—an object which fortunately was successfully countered by a strong force of French and British cavalry.

"Where is the Hussar who carried this message?" asked the General.

"He is dead, sir," replied Danby. "He was pursued and shot by Uhlans, of whom we managed to kill several and to drive off the rest."

"Dead, is he?"

"Yes, sir, and when he was dying, he asked that the dispatch-case might be brought on to you at once," said the patrol-leader.

"And who are you, my lad?" asked the General, kindly.

"Oscar Danby of Maxwell's Eagles, sir, detailed for duty with the 13th Brigade," replied Danby, with not a little touch of pride in his voice.

"Maxwell's Eagles, eh?" replied the great soldier, smiling.

"Yes, sir."

"Then you're the boys who caught the German spy on the East Coast at the outbreak of war, aren't you?"

The youths blushingly acknowledged that they had had that piece of good fortune.

"H'm! that was some capture.   He was a master craftsman, that fellow."

Danby and Bancroft looked at each other in some amazement.   This was high praise from a General of the British Army.

"You are both brave lads, and you have rendered me a great service by bringing this dispatch.   I have already heard of Maxwell's Eagles, and right well they deserve their name.   I shall hope to hear of you again," said the General.

Then the lads saluted, and departed out of the great man's presence, feeling tired and hungry but very happy.

CHAPTER XVI.

THE BATTLE IN THE CLOUDS.

It was during the Battle of the Aisne, after the Germans had been hurled back from the River Marne, that the Eagles came once more into active touch with the enemy. For some two or three weeks previous to this they had been rendering good service in the rear of the French and British lines. All sorts of duties had fallen to their lot, and they had toiled cheerfully, often for forty-eight hours without sleep, carrying dispatches, stretcher-bearing, serving as camp orderlies about the head-quarters, and doing a hundred and one things that a boy can do just as well as a man.

On two occasions, at least, Danby and Willoughby had carried wounded officers and men, out of the line of fire, down to the waiting motor ambulances in the rear. In burning heat, rain, mud and slush they had toiled, until

(167)

their faces were bronzed and weather-beaten. And always their presence was welcomed by the soldiers, who had come to regard them as their friends.

"Bravo, Maxwell's Eagles!" the soldiers would say, if one of them happened to join a camp-fire or bivouac, or pass by the billets on some errand.

Even the French soldiers had learnt to love them, and would often give a complimentary salute, sometimes adding:—

"Voila, les aigles de Maxwell. Vive les braves garcons Anglais!"

It was during the fighting around Soissons and Chavonne, when the British troops, in the face of fearful artillery and machine-gun fire, crossed the Aisne, partly by boats at Chavonne and partly by clambering across the broken girders of the bridge at Pont-Arcy, that Danby had his first flight on a biplane. It happened as follows:—

The Eagles were posted a little in the rear of the attacking columns of the 4th and 5th Brigades of the First Army Corps under General Sir Douglas Haig, when one of the lads noticed a biplane returning from the high ground about Moussy and Chavonne on the enemy's side of the river.

At first they thought it to be a Taube coming over from the enemy's lines to reconnoitre, until Willoughby suddenly exclaimed :—

"Look at that biplane. It must be English, else why are the Germans firing at it."

"So it is. I can see the red, white and blue rings on the under-side of the planes," replied Shackleton.

"A warm time he must be having up there. The shrapnel is bursting all around him," cried Danby. "It must be jolly exciting."

"See, he's hit!" cried another, as the biplane swerved suddenly, nose-dived a little, then rapidly recovering itself, continued its journey towards the Allied lines and safety.

Nearer and nearer it came, as they watched it eagerly, forgetting for a moment the fighting down below. And indeed it was a thrilling sight to watch the little machine heading its way through the white puffs of bursting shell.

"Hullo! he's coming down, boys. I wonder what's the matter," cried John Holland.

The next moment the machine made a downward glide, for the engine had been shut off, and in a couple of minutes more it came to earth not fifty yards from where they were standing.

"Look, he's hailing us. There are two men in it and I believe one of them's wounded," said one of the lads.

"Eagles! Quick march—Double!" ordered the chief.

"Anything wrong?" cried the scout-master as the patrol raced up.

"Yes, my wireless operator has been hit by a shrapnel bullet. Will you take charge of him, as I must go back again."

"Certainly."

"Bring up the stretcher, Willoughby and Bancroft, and be quick. The man's fainted."

Then, while John Holland rendered first-aid to the wounded man, the air pilot asked one of the others who stood by to start the propeller, saying that he must go back again to reconnoitre some big gun positions on the other side of the river.

As he jumped back into his seat, he half-turned round and said :—

"You're Maxwell's Eagles, aren't you?"

"Yes, sir," replied the youths, who were overjoyed at this opportunity of assisting a member of the Royal Flying Corps on active service.

"I hear you're a smart lot. Any of you know how to manage a 'wireless'?"

"Yes, sir. Danby here knows all about it. In fact he's an expert at the job," came the instant reply.

"Indeed. Which is Danby?"

"This is Danby. He's our patrol-leader," exclaimed the others.

"Ever been up in a plane, Danby?"

"No, sir."

"Would you like to go?"

"Wouldn't I just, sir!" exclaimed the blushing lad.

"And you wouldn't be afraid?"

"I don't think so."

"Could you manage to send a few letters on the wireless, do you think?"

"Yes, sir. Quite easily."

"Jump in, then—that is, if your chief will permit you."

Danby looked at Holland. Just one appealing look. For a few seconds the chief hesitated to give his consent. It was a dangerous thing, but still, if Danby wished it, why should he hold him back. He had been in more dangerous positions before, and would be again before the month was out. He nodded his assent, saying:—

"Be careful, then, Danby."

"Thank you, sir!" cried the excited youth, and the next instant he was in the observer's seat, just behind the pilot, and looking over his shoulder.

"Now start the propeller, one of you," and the next instant Shackleton, exerting his strength, set the blades whirling. The great machine slid forward over the little patch of level ground which had been selected for alighting, as it had the advantage of being sheltered behind a hillock. Faster and faster it went, then it left the ground.

"Good-bye, Danby, and good luck!" cried the others, waving their hats, as the machine rose higher and higher.

"Good-bye, Eagles!" came back the answer faintly and seemingly already far away.

For one awful moment the brave youth felt as if he had acted foolishly. Recovering his usual composure, however, he gripped one of the stays of the biplane tightly, and prepared himself for what was to come.

"All right?" queried the pilot, jerking his head sideway to get a glance at his passenger. "Not frightened, are you?"

"Not a bit," answered Danby, trying to shake off that first gruesome feeling that possessed him, as they left the earth behind, though it was with difficulty that they could hear one another owing to the noise of the propeller.

Higher and higher they climbed, until even the sound of the heavy artillery on both sides of the Aisne seemed to fade away, but always in their ears was the roaring of those whirling blades, so that only by shouting could they hear one another speak.

Now the whole battle-field was open beneath them. The winding river where the British troops were forcing a crossing, the broken bridge at Pont-Arcy, and the bridge of boats at Chavonne, were all laid out like a miniature map beneath them. It was scarcely possible to define the attacking parties, however, unless they moved in some close column or dense mass.

On they went, right over the enemy's lines, searching for those hidden gun positions, from whence the enemy were harassing the Allied crossing. The sheer fascination of flying had gripped Danby, so that he no longer feared to look down. Suddenly, he became aware of some strange thing that was happening:—

"Puff-whiff! Puff-whiff!"

What were those white puffs of smoke all around them? And what was that evil-smelling stuff that nearly choked him, every now and again?

"Swish—splosh!" came something, that splintered the framework to which he held. Not till then did he realize that they had become the target for a score of guns far down below. The sound of the engine and propeller had prevented him from hearing the bursting of the shrapnel, and it was not till the splinters began to fly about him, and he saw a trickle of blood ooze down his fingers that he knew they were the centre of a hail-storm of lead.

But still they sailed on and on, past the first and second line trenches of the enemy. Then they were out of danger for a while.

"Keep a good look-out for their big guns!" yelled the pilot.

Then they dropped down a little, and searched the earth beneath them carefully for the big flashes. Soon, they found the spot whence came those huge 16-inch shells that worried the Allies.

"Are you ready?" cried the pilot, who was keenly noting where the English shells fell, that were trying to hit the heavy batteries beneath them.

"Yes," shouted back the youth, his fingers on the keys of the little transmitter.

"Two hundred—left!" and the message was sent. Then the machine circled around a little, while the pilot watched the effect of the changed fire.

"One hundred—right!" came next, then soon after, "Fifty—left." Two minutes later, "Direct Hit," was signalled, as one big gun was silenced and most of the gunners killed. And so the work went on, until Danby, looking down, espied far beneath them a couple of Taubes climbing up to attack them.

"Enemy planes ascending!" he shouted as

hard as he could. The pilot heard and understood.

Like a bird of prey the biplane wheeled round and started back, for she had no gun, being only a swift scouter. Away she went, pursued by the Taubes. And then to make matters worse, another enemy plane was observed in front of them, and somewhat higher. She was armed and was preparing to fire.

It was now a question of manœuvring, and Jelks, who was one of the most skilful pilots of the R.F.C., performed gymnastic gyrations and contortions, as though he were an acrobat in mid-air performing monkey tricks for a delighted crowd below.

" Hold tight ! " he would yell, as he prepared for another nose-dive, or a more violent contortion, for the enemy in front had begun to fire. Then the splinters began to fly again. The planes were pierced in a score of places by bullets. Several more ribs were broken. But so far the engine, petrol tanks and propeller had escaped, though at any moment they might go.

They were close upon the enemy now, and he was still firing rapidly, but a clever nose-dive right under the German gave them peace for a moment. Now he had all the three planes behind him, and the pilot hoped by his superior speed to give them the slip. Another minute and he jerked his head back to look upon his foes.

Yes, he was leaving them, and their fire was less accurate. They had still the enemy's front lines to cross, however, and to face the shrapnel once more. Could they do it? The pilot looked anxiously at his machine. It was rapidly becoming a wreck, though so far no vital part had been hit. He could not afford to lose any more stays, however. Now they were in the midst of it once again. Puff-puff! came the shells. They were sailing through clouds of evil-smelling and poisonous gas, when :—

"Crash!" came a shell right into the engine, and for a moment they were both blinded and staggered. The machine rocked violently. The engine and propellers had stopped, for they had been shivered to pieces. The pilot's left arm was hanging limp and disabled. Then, Danby caught sight of his pale, determined face for an instant, as he half-turned, and called :—

" Are you hurt much, Danby ? "

" Not much, sir," the lad managed to say, though his head was in a whirl.

They were falling now, or rather planing over the enemy's front trenches, for, with the engine gone, there was nothing left but to glide down, for luckily the planes still served them, though they were pierced in a hundred places. The rudders, too, were not finally done for.

" Danby," called the pilot faintly now, for the whirr of the propeller having ceased, it was possible to hear.

" Yes, sir," answered the lad, trying to pull himself together.

" I am blind ! "

" Blind ? " wailed the youth, realizing the hopelessness of their position.

" Yes, but I can manage to steer, if you give me the directions. Guide me to the spot where we started from. It cannot be far away now. Can you see it ? "

" Yes, sir," replied Danby. " We have passed the enemy's lines now. There it is, a little to the right. Shall I hold the joy-stick ? "

" No. Give me the direction and I can

manage," but the voice came fainter and fainter.

It seemed an eternity to Oscar as they descended, but gradually they drew nearer and nearer to the spot. There were the Eagles waving to them.

"Left a little! Right a wee bit! Now we're there. A hundred feet—fifty!" and with a crash the machine came to the earth within a hundred yards from the starting-place.

Danby remembered nothing more after that crash until three days later he came to himself. He was lying in a bed at the base hospital, some ten or fifteen miles behind the lines, and the first face that he saw was that of John Holland, bending over him.

The serious face of the scout-master relaxed into a smile as the lad opened his eyes.

"Where am I, sir?" asked Oscar.

"You are at the base hospital having a rest," replied the kind voice of the chief.

The voice of John Holland sounded strange and hollow in the ears of Danby. He thought he was sailing far away over distant seas, and the waves were speaking to him. Again and again he murmured :—

" Where am I ?   Who are you ? "

Poor lad, his mind was wandering, but he was struggling and fighting his way back to consciousness slowly.   He seemed to have left the world far beneath him, and at times every sound resolved itself into the voice of the waves, or the whir-r-r of an aeroplane engine ; yet there seemed to be music and rhythm in it all, and through it all, again and again, the face of John Holland seemed to float amid the haze.

Danby's gallant and devoted act was not permitted to pass unrecorded, for, later in the day, it came to the ears of the Divisional Commander, who ordered it to be mentioned in the Divisional Orders next morning.   And two days afterwards, while Danby still lay unconscious, and apparently very near to the border-land, the Commander-in-Chief rode over to the hospital, and in accordance with his powers of General Officer Commanding on the Field, he awarded and bestowed, in the name of the King, that most coveted of all decorations, the Victoria Cross, upon both Danby and the pilot.

Days went by, but at length youth and

a vigorous constitution conquered, and his strength came back a little, and he began to look around him with more apparent interest.

"And this—what is this, sir?" asked the lad, playing with a little gun-metal cross attached to his shirt by a ribbon.

"Oh, that is the Victoria Cross, which the Commander-in-Chief pinned on your breast when he came to see you."

"The Victoria Cross? But I don't remember anyone coming to see me?"

"No, you were asleep, and we dared not wake you, so he kissed you and pinned it on to your shirt."

Then with a thrill Danby remembered it all —that terrible battle in the clouds, and the aerial flight through the bursting shrapnel, over the enemy's lines flashed before his eyes once more. He saw it all again, and heard the brave pilot's words :—

"Danby—I am blind!"

Then, turning to John Holland, the lad said :—

"And the pilot, where is he?"

"Alas, he will never fly again, for he is blind ; hopelessly blind in both eyes. How you came to earth without being killed is a mystery to all of us, but the pilot says you were brave and calm to the end, and that you served him as well as his own observer, and sent the messages correctly. And after he was hit, you directed him how to steer. You came to earth with a bit of a crash, for the machine could hold out no longer; there were more than a hundred bullet holes through it, besides shrapnel. The pilot has also been similarly decorated, and has received in addition a pension for life, as he can never fly again."

Danby sank back on to the bed from which he had partly raised himself. He was feverish, and there was a hectic flush on his cheeks and brow, but in his eyes there was a gleam of joy, while a faint smile suffused itself over his features.

And so, fondling the treasured medallion with his hand, he fell asleep once more, and in that sweet restful sleep he found the strength and vigour he would need for the coming days.

And this was how Oscar Danby, of the Eagle Patrol, won the V.C.

CHAPTER XVII.

THE BATTLE OF YPRES.

FORTUNATELY, Danby's injuries were not very serious. He had been badly bruised and shaken when the aeroplane fell to the earth, but after a fortnight in the hospital and a few days spent at Wimereux on the French coast as a convalescent, he was declared fit for service again, and shortly afterwards he rejoined his patrol.

It was during the Allied advance towards Belgium, when the fighting was very fierce, and many villages were taken and retaken by both sides, and the tide of battle ebbed and flowed, that the Eagles next saw real service.

It was the 30th of October, 1914, when the Germans, bringing all their heavy artillery into action, made another great attempt for the Channel ports. The advanced British divisions were holding the salient at the Gheluvelt cross-roads, where there is a little Belgian village a few miles to the east of Ypres.

The German Emperor himself was with his men, and he had told them that the winning of the Channel ports would mean the end of the war, because England, the most hated foe of all, would then be at their mercy.

Soon after daylight, the position had become extremely serious, for the British trenches had been pounded to pieces. Some of the companies were actually buried alive, while a division on the British right, holding the ground in front of Klein Zillebeke, had to fall back a trifle. Then it was that the enemy, discovering a gap, made their great onslaught. Five German Army Corps were hurled in waves against the thin British line. It was not a case of three or four to one, but, as one participant has said :—

" It was more like eight to one."

General Sir Douglas Haig, realizing the grave danger that threatened the little British Army, had ordered :—

" The cross-roads at Gheluvelt, and the line of the canal, must be held at all costs."

And never did troops respond with a greater

courage, or make a nobler sacrifice than did the English Brigades that day. Backwards and forwards the line of battle swayed. Sometimes a battalion was cut off, and fought surrounded for hours, as did the Royal Scots Fusiliers, who, when the fight was over, showed up a muster roll of seventy men under one subaltern, out of a complement of a thousand.

It was during this terrible fight that the lads of the Eagle Patrol once more rendered a great service to the British Army. They had been busy with the stretchers, carrying the wounded to the rear, and the shells were falling all around them, when they saw a dispatch rider racing towards them at full speed, amid a whirl of dust and the smoke of bursting shells. As he passed the lads, he reined in a little, and yelled :—

"Hullo! Are you Maxwell's Eagles?"

"Yes," they cried.

"Then for God's sake lend a hand, if you can!"

"What can we do?" replied the Eagles, putting down their empty stretchers, with which they were returning to the front lines.

"Do? Why, everything," shouted the man.

"One of our most trusted Belgian guides has just misled us, and there's a devil of a mess up there."

"Oh, what is the matter? Was he a spy?"

"Yes, the devil was in the pay of the Germans. He managed to get some false orders delivered to one of the battalions, and there's a gap through which the Bosches are pouring. They've caught him, though, the rascal. They put him up against a tree and riddled him with bullets in a trice. But what we want now is men—men—men at once!"

"Right oh!" cried the Eagles. "Where can we get them from?"

"Anywhere. Sprint as fast as you can. Bring up the cooks, Army Service Corps men, water-carriers, anyone, at once. The telephone wires have been cut by shrapnel. I'm off to carry the message to any reserves I can find. Scoot now, or the battle's lost. Order them all up to that line of willows over there. I'm off!"

And with that the horseman, who had gabbled all this off in less than a minute, dug his spurs into the flank of his horse and disappeared round a bend in the road.

"Leave the stretchers, Eagles!" ordered Danby, the patrol-leader, who acted as chief, for they had left Holland in the trenches, dealing with urgent cases.

There could be no doubt as to the truth of this news, for the tide of battle rolled nearer and nearer. Even the line of willows and hedges less than a mile away was blurred by flashes and bursting shells, while the cheering and counter-cheering of the troops, and even the clash of steel as the men fought hand to hand in the trenches and over the parapets, could be distinctly heard.

"Scatter round, Eagles! Double up, and bring in assistance!" cried Danby, waiting no longer.

Then each lad took a bee-line for the nearest billets, tents and huts behind the lines, and requested cooks, camp-followers, water-carriers and every one they met to come to the assistance of the hard-pressed men who were holding the front line against such fearful odds. Even odd parties of French cuirassiers, with their silver helmets and steel breastplates, rode up in response to the summons, dismounted and joined with their sabres in a bayonet fight, for every one soon realized the seriousness of the position.

Men came up in all sorts of attire, without caps, coats, and puttees, and took a hand in the fight. This it was, and the gallant stand of the Fusiliers, who would not retire but sacrificed themselves, that saved Ypres that day. For by this the ground was held until help came from the second division, which had been posted to the north of Gheluvelt, and had not been very much engaged that morning.

During that fateful day the brigades became very much mixed, and next day, when the battle began again, the lads found themselves with the Worcesters, one of the most famous regiments in the British Army ; a regiment which had won its laurels a hundred years ago under Wellington in the Peninsula.

During the night the English lines had been reformed somewhat, and strengthened. The ugly gap between the Seventh Division and the Second Brigade had been filled by dismounted cavalry.

Dawn was once more the signal for a terrible outburst of artillery. The British took what cover they could in the newly-dug trenches and dug-outs, for the little village had been abandoned for a while when the new formations were made.

"They're a-comin' on agen!" cried a soldier, who watched through a periscope as soon as the artillery slackened.

"Stand ready, Worcesters!" came the order.

Then as Danby peeped through a periscope, he saw a wave of grey uniforms coming up in close formation. And beyond that was a second wave, and a third. He did not look for more.

"Worcesters—Rapid fire!" came the order, and from the whole length of the trench a spurt of flame went out, accompanied by a leaden hail of bullets. Then the rattle of machine-guns accompanied the crackle of the rifles—

"Rip-r-r-r-r-r-r!"

Down went the first German wave, like corn before the reaper, while over the heads of the men in the trenches, the French "Seventy-fives" and the British "Eighteen-pounders" screamed and ploughed through the ranks of the second wave. But still the Germans came on, over the prostrate forms of the first ranks,

singing something that sounded like a melan-
choly dirge.

Danby and Bancroft, standing up between a
corporal and a private of the Worcesters,
emptied their fifteen rounds with the rest.
Then, when their rifles had become so hot
that it was impossible to hold them, they laid
them down for a while, till the third wave came
up, bringing back with it the remnants of the
first and second lines that had escaped the
withering fire.

"Steady, lads! Take it coolly!" the commander kept saying, as he paced the trench
with a cane in his hand and a lighted cigarette
in his mouth.

Then followed another brief lull till the next
wave came within effective range.

"Got a woodbine, Bill?" one soldier would
say to his chum. "Thanks, old man. Just
got time for another whiff, afore the blighters
come on!"

A moment later, the range-finder was heard
to call out :—

"Six hundred yards — Five - fifty — Five
hundred!"

Then again came the order to fire, and

fifteen seconds later "Rapid fire." Suddenly, as the broken lines of the enemy surged on and came to within seventy yards of the trench, the colonel shouted :—

"Worcesters—Fix bayonets—Charge !"

With a wild cheer, the men sprang over the parapets ; a long line of steel glinted in the sun, and with a swoop like a hawk they dashed forward to meet that already wavering line of grey-blue.   Then was seen with what a terrible strength and majesty the British soldier fights.

Nothing could stop them.   All the disciplined valour and stability of the best Prussian and Bavarian troops disappeared before that ter- rific charge.   They swept the enemy before them like chaff.   He did not even stay to fight, but fled before that on-coming wave of khaki. The whole German line was pierced, rolled up, and disappeared.   Hundreds of prisoners were taken.

Then the Worcesters were formed up for a breather on the captured ground, and before the German artillery could readjust the range, they swept forward again.   On they went to the cross-roads which they had abandoned the day before.   Even here they stayed only until the Cavalry Brigade, coming up at the gallop, cleared the woods on their flank of the enemy's sharp-shooters, and the Oxford Light Infantry came up to their aid. Then their colonel cried out :—

"Bravo, Worcesters! Nothing can stop you. Now the village, lads. Let's clear the village. Forward—Charge!"

And with another British cheer the men sprang forward, and with them went the Eagles. Danby and Bancroft became separated from the rest, and entered the village with the first group. A fierce fire from hidden machine-guns met them, and from loop-holes in the houses and other buildings rifles crackled, but nothing could withstand the desperate courage of the Worcesters. Hand to hand they fought in the streets; step by step they cleared the houses of their opponents; but the carnage was dreadful. Dead and wounded, friend and foe, were inextricably mixed up in that violent combat.

For a time the Eagles were in a position of great peril. Half a battalion of Prussian Guards with three machine-guns blocked the street in front of the Worcesters and made a valiant stand to cover the now inevitable retreat of their Brigade.

For ten minutes the fighting was so desperate and evenly balanced that no progress could be made. Then above the roar of the guns and the clash of steel, a cry was heard :—

"Make way for the guns!"

A minute later half a battery of the Royal Horse Artillery galloped up, unlimbered and opened fire in double quick-time upon the Prussians.

In three minutes a gap was made in those serried ranks ; then, as the breach widened, the skirl of the pipes was heard, and with a wild cheer two companies of Highlanders, coming up, charged through the guns, and got home with the bayonet, effectually clearing a way.

During the fiercest portion of the fight no quarter was asked and none given. Then, as the passions of the men died down, great bunches of prisoners were taken, and when the enemy was finally driven from the village, the Eagles joined in the work of rescue.

John Holland had at last found all his band, save one. Shackleton was missing.

"Where could he be?" they asked each other, as they carried the wounded men to the houses, and tended them while the stretchers came up.

They had been engaged on this work for some little time, when Bancroft, coming upon a heap of dead and wounded that almost blocked the roadway, shouted :—

"Here he is!   Eagles, lend a hand!"

CHAPTER XVIII.

A BRUTAL FOE.

CAREFULLY, and with great tenderness, the Eagles removed the pile of dead and wounded men, and last of all they came to Shackleton. They called him by name, they shook him gently, but, alas, he was dead. The smile of victory was upon his fair, upturned face, which was marred only by a thin streak of blood from a bullet wound in the forehead.

"Shackleton!" they still called, for they could not bring themselves to believe that he was dead. But no reply came from those pale lips.

Then for a moment a wave of emotion swept over the troop. Even Danby's eyes swam with a thick mist, and everything became blurred and indistinct. Could it really be that their chum had passed away for ever, and would never speak to them again? It was a bitter moment for them. Something of the glory of victory faded away; they had paid for it too dearly. Even John Holland, as he looked upon the lad's face, could scarcely restrain his feelings. At that moment he would gladly have given his own life to bring Shackleton back again. But it could not be. Death had laid its icy hand upon the patrol and had claimed its first victim.

Knowing, however, that regrets could not help matters, and seeing much work remained to be done in attending to the wounded, Holland recalled the lads to their duty :—

"Eagles," he said, "it's a sad day for the patrol. This is our first loss; I pray God that it may be our last," and the lads, with bended heads, responded in their hearts, if not with their lips, "Amen!"

"But he has died like a hero, fighting in a just cause; and by this time he has received his reward. He has followed the great Pathfinder into the unknown, and now he is at rest. But come, Eagles," went on the scout-master, "let us not be too sad; there is much work to be done. Let us give a hand with the wounded."

Thus did John Holland draw the lads back

from their grief to a sense of duty. And when they had laid the body of their comrade gently aside, until they had time to inter him decently, they returned to their work.

So for an hour or more they tended the wounded, both English and Germans, giving water from their own scanty store to the thirsty ; bandaging wounds, carrying stretchers, and making the lot of many a poor fellow easier and more comfortable. Carefully they straightened out the limbs of the dead, and carried them away for burial. Many a terrible sight they saw, but they allowed not their finer feelings to clash with their duty.

"Ach, Himmel! Kamerad, wasser—wasser zu trinken!" cried a dying German, as they passed on their errand of mercy, and immediately Danby was at the poor fellow's side, and pouring the last few remaining drops of water from his own bottle down the man's throat, though he himself was so parched with dust and heat that he could scarcely speak.

"Ich danke ihnen," whispered the dying man, for he had forgotten all his hatred, and his blue eyes beamed the thanks he could scarcely utter.

Then, as the water revived him a little, his voice became stronger, and he asked :—

"Sprechen sie Deutsch, mein herr ?"

At these words, Danby shook his head to indicate that he did not speak German, but, seeing John Holland near by, he called him to the man's side, and said :—

"I think, sir, that this poor fellow wants to give some message to be forwarded, perhaps to his wife. Will you give him a few moments ? I don't think he can live long."

"Certainly I will, Danby," replied the other, and a moment afterwards he was bending over the dying man, and taking the last farewell message to his wife and child.

At that moment a burst of artillery fire came from the edge of the wood just a little way outside the village. Then wild shouts were heard and the tramp, tramp of armed men. The Germans were counter-attacking in great force and were determined to capture the ruined village once again.

"Stand firm, boys ! Give it 'em, lads !" cried an officer, who commanded the advanced British companies. Then a moment later, as the spatter of the rifles and the rip-r-r-r of the machine-guns began, a voice called :—

"Worcesters—fix bay'nets—charge !"

And away went the first three companies clean through the lines of the advancing Bosches, but the gallant few, though they sacrificed themselves almost to a man, in order to allow the other regiments time to fall back and reform, were overwhelmed by the masses of the approaching enemy.

Twice also the Cavalry Brigade charged the German ranks, using the lance and sabre with deadly effect, then, wheeling sharply round, fought their way back, and galloped to the cross-roads, where the next stand was to be made.

In the height of all this confusion, the Eagles had remained at their task of succouring the wounded. It was all done so quickly that there was little time to comprehend what was happening. Even John Holland, not apprehending that the Germans were in force, had remained by the dying man. Suddenly, he was surrounded by wildly excited German troops, and a patrol of Uhlans galloping up at that moment surrounded the Eagles, and

threatened them with death unless they sur
rendered.

One burly fellow, springing from his horse,
and seeing the scout-master holding the expir-
ing German, with several souvenirs in his hand
which he had promised the dying man to forward to his wife, charged him with robbing a
wounded comrade.

John Holland sprang to his feet at this dire
insult, and told the Uhlan in his own language
what he thought of him.

"I have been taking messages from the poor
fellow," he said, "and have promised to forward to his wife these few trifles as a keep-
sake."

"He speaks not the truth," cried another
Uhlan, while yet another, hearing Holland
speak the German tongue so well, added :—

"A spy—er ist einer spaher ! Let us shoot
the verdomt Englander !"

"Agreed !" they all shouted together.
"Let the dog die. What matters it ? It will
only be an English spy the less."

"Very well," replied John Holland calmly,
looking his captors bravely in the face.
"Shoot me if you like. Only promise me that

you will not harm these boys. It is my fault they are here ; they stayed with me to succour the wounded when our own troops retired."

"Was that the reason why you stayed be-hind, when your brave Britishers ran off as fast as their legs could carry them ? " asked a lieutenant of Uhlans who had just come up and heard this last part of the speech, which was also delivered in German.

"I give you my word that it is so," replied the scout-master to this man, who had a most brutal and cruel face, and was moreover partly under the influence of drink.

"Ach ! " exclaimed the lieutenant, spitting in Holland's face. "What is an Englishman's word worth ? You stayed behind to spy."

"You lie, sir ! " cried the captive, whose hands were now bound behind his back. "If I were free, you would answer that insult with your life. And as to an Englishman's word, sir . . . it is not a scrap of paper. It is some-thing for which he is prepared to give his life."

"Then give your life for it, you infernal British dog ! " hissed the German between his teeth, for Holland's words had cut him like a knife.

Instantly turning to his men, who had dismounted and tied up the rest of the Eagles, he shouted :—

" Firing squad, fall in—ten paces back there ! " and the Uhlans fell in as requested, loaded their rifles and held them at the ready.

" Tie that man to a tree there, dachshunds ! " he commanded next, for he treated even his own men with the utmost contempt.

Then it was that the Eagles, realizing for the first time the imminent danger in which their chief stood, and knowing the brutal temperament of some German officers, feared the worst. What could they do ? There was not a moment to waste. They themselves were now tied by their hands to the bridles or saddles of the mounted Uhlans, who stood about in a rough semicircle, for by this time the tide of battle had drifted beyond the village to the cross-roads once again.

" Do not kill Mr. Holland, sir ! " pleaded MacGregor, one of the younger lads.

" Hold your tongue ! " cried the Uhlan to whose bridle he was tied, striking him at the same time a smart blow across the head with the shaft of his lance.

" He was only assisting your wounded, sir,"
urged Danby. "Do not shoot him ; he is a
good man."

"How do I know he is a good man ?"
snapped the brutal lieutenant, who evidently
understood English. "I tell you he is a
spy, and my orders are to shoot all spies at
sight."

"But ask your own wounded. Ask that
dying man over there, whom you charge him
with robbing."

"How can I when he is dead, you dog?
Probably he killed the man as well as robbed
him. Just keep a civil tongue in your head,
or it will be your turn next."

"Are you ready there, dogs ?" asked the
officer of the troopers who had been tying up
John Holland, and placing a handkerchief
across his eyes.

"Ja wohl, mein herr," replied the sergeant,
"we are ready," and the men sprang back a
few paces.

" Firing squad, present——"

"You shall not murder Mr. Holland, you
villains !" cried MacGregor, breaking away
from his captor, and springing forward until

he covered the scout-master with his own body.

"Stay there at your peril, you young scamp!" shouted the enraged lieutenant, waving back the troopers who would have pulled the lad away.

"I will stay here at my peril; I am not afraid to die," cried the laddie.

"Then you shall die also. Tie a handkerchief over his eyes, sergeant."

"No, I want no handkerchief. I'm no feard o' the flash o' your rifles!" replied MacGregor, breaking out for the last time into his native doric.

"Go away, MacGregor, quickly, or they'll shoot you also," urged the scout-master, who, though blindfolded, felt the lad's presence in front of him. But the lad moved not nor spake again.

"Quick now. We're wasting time over these English devils. If the youngster won't move, let him die. Stand back there a little."

"Firing squad, present—fire!" came the order.

From the barrels of the six rifles there came a jet of flame, and the leaden messengers of death, and before Danby and the three remaining Eagles could realize what was happening, John Holland and MacGregor lay dead upon the ground.   Death was instantaneous, and the Scotch laddie's head lay across the breast of his brave leader.

Stupefied and bewildered, the lads looked helplessly on.   They were powerless to avert the terrible tragedy which had befallen them. They had never dreamed that such a thing could be possible.   Surely it was but a terrible nightmare they were passing through, and presently they would awake!

Alas, it was no dream, for there on the ground lay the lifeless and blood-stained form of John Holland, the man they loved most on earth, and beside him, locked in the slumber of death, lay MacGregor, their school-chum and comrade-in-arms.

"Oh, God, that it could have happened!" was all that escaped from Danby's lips, as, for the first time in his life, he fell fainting to the ground.

So died John Holland, one of the bravest and truest men who ever lived.   He died a victim to German hatred and malice.   He might have saved his life had he left the wounded German to suffer and die, but in that case he would have lost his honour, and to John Holland this would have been worse than death.

An English gentleman and a chivalrous soldier, his spirit still lives on in the brave lads who survived him, and though he sleeps in a little orchard across the sea, yet he laid down his life for a sacred cause, and wherever the story of "Maxwell's Eagles" shall be told, there also will men hear of that brave and chivalrous man—John Holland.

CHAPTER XIX.

THE LOST PATROL.

WHEN Danby recovered consciousness, he found himself and his three companions, Bancroft, Willoughby and Murphy, being transported on a damaged gun-limber to the rear of the German lines. These four lads were now all who remained of the Eagle Patrol, and they knew not as yet whether their fate would be similar to that which had been meted out to the others. At present, however, they were simply prisoners of war. Whether they were to be tried by court-martial and shot, they knew not; neither did they care much, for death had lost all its horrors for them.

They had seen John Holland die a cruel and unjust death, and MacGregor, the laddie from Auld Reekie, who had been their close companion for three years, had bravely chosen to die with him.

"Oh, God, better if we had all died together!" moaned Danby, for at his heart there was a dull aching pain. And his head was in a continual whirl. It seemed as though he was just waking from a bad dream. Sometimes he consoled himself with thinking that it was only a dream that he was passing through, and that he would awake soon, and find things all right again.

"John Holland dead?" he would ask himself. "MacGregor dead? No, it could not be." He raised his head and looked around as though expecting to meet the eyes of his chief, but instead he saw the pale face and gleaming eyes of Bancroft and the others who were all tied fast to the limber beside him. They had evidently been passing through the same bitter experiences. They had lost their best friend, and they would never see his like again.

Suddenly, Danby heard some one call him faintly. It was young Willoughby, just behind him, and he was saying :—

"Danby, have you a drop of water left in your bottle? I am parched and ready to die with thirst."

The patrol-leader felt for his bottle ; it was empty. Now he remembered having given the last drop to the dying German, who had begged it for the love of heaven.

"Sorry, Willoughby, old man. I haven't a drop left, or you should have it." Then, remembering the words of the German who had appealed to him for water, he repeated them as nearly as he could to one of the escort, a Prussian infantry-man who walked beside the wheel of the gun-carriage.

"Ach, Himmel! Wasser zu trinken!" he said, pointing to his parched mouth, and to that of his comrade. But the Prussian replied brusquely :—

"No water to spare!"

So they were perforce compelled to ride on and endure their thirst as well as they could. A little later in the day, however, they came to a fountain, where the water gushed out on the roadside, and a fair-haired Saxon, who formed one of the escort, which was a mixed company, came up and said quietly to the scouts :—

"Lend me your water-bottles, and I will fill them here while we are resting. I know you English Scouts ; you are honourable, and you always do at least one kind deed each day to

some one.   I have lived in London ten years,
and once my leetle brother was fetched out of
the Regent's Canal by one of your boy scouts.
I will do this thing for you, to show you that
all ze Germans are not bad."

"A thousand thanks!" said Danby, un-
fastening his water-bottle, and smiling weakly.

A moment later the four boys were taking
long drinks of the cool, refreshing water.   Then
the Saxon filled them again, despite the scowl
of the Prussian, who had noticed him.

"Thank God, that at least one of our captors
has a kind heart," whispered Danby to the
others.

"Yes," replied Bancroft, "let us buck up,
and take courage.   We may have a chance to
slip away from the brutes when darkness
comes.   We must rely upon you now, Danby;
you are our leader; we have no other."

At these words a new light leapt into
Danby's eyes, and a new spirit seemed to pervade him.   Whether it was that precious cold
water which had revived him, or whether
Bancroft's words had something to do with it,
I cannot say.   Perhaps it was both.   At any
rate, from that moment he was a different

personality. Although a prisoner, with death maybe staring him in the face, he was now leader of the Eagle Patrol, which had already won for itself a name both in England and in France.

By God's help he determined to rise to the occasion. He would never lose his courage or hope again. He would be courteous to his jailors, but he would not cringe before them. If need be, he would die like John Holland, and face the firing squad without a shudder. He felt just a trifle ashamed of his past weakness, if such it could be called, but he would never quail again, not even before the Prussian War Lord himself. If they were imprisoned or interned, then he, the leader of the Eagle Patrol, would contrive some method of escape, and once free they would soon be over the border, for did he not carry at this moment a map of Western Germany and the Rhine between the inner and outer sole of his boot.

Ah, yes, he would wait patiently, even cheerfully, and see what these Prussians meant to do with them. It would all come right in the end. He only regretted one thing, and that was, that it was not in his power to avenge the death of that good and innocent man, John Holland, upon that coarse and brutal lieutenant of Uhlans.

Had he known it, however, his mind could have been at rest upon this point, for that unworthy murderer had already met his fate at the hands of the British troops, and this is how it happened.

When the English Brigades fell back to reform at the cross-roads, owing to the sudden pressure of the German hordes, they made but a short halt. Six times already they had captured and lost the village, and they waited but a little while for their reserves to come up before they made another attempt. As soon therefore as the Highlanders came up to strengthen the Worcesters and the Oxford Light Infantry, the order was given to advance.

And never was a command more willingly obeyed. The men were keen, and moreover, they knew that many of their wounded had been left in German hands, and more than once they had heard dark tales of how their wounded had been treated by the Bosche.

" The Brigade will deploy, then advance by
short rushes and retake the village!" was the
order which came through, and was received
by cheering.

Advancing in open formation, they soon
drove in the enemy's snipers and outposts.
Then, once again, the order came :—

" Fix bay'nets—charge !"

And now for the seventh time the village
of Gheluvelt was in the hands of the British,
though street fighting continued for another
hour.   At first, fiercely, then it slacked off to a
little desultory fighting.   As the Highlanders
and the Worcesters dashed into the village,
one of the latter came across the body of John
Holland, lying in a pool of blood beside a
tree, and resting on it, as though in sleep, was
the corpse of MacGregor.

" See this, mate ?" yelled the soldier, who
was the corporal with whose section the Eagles
had served only that morning, when the companies had been so mixed up.

" What is it, corporal ?" asked the other,
resting the butt of his smoking rifle on the
ground for a moment, in order to regain his
breath.

"This man has been shot as a spy. Look at the 'ankerchief round his napper. An' it's one o' Maxwell's Eagles. He ain't no spy!"

"Blimey, Bill, that he ain't! He's the bloke wot stayed behind to dress the wounded. He's the leader o' them Eagle boys."

"An' here's one of his boys shot through the head too," cried another soldier.

"Smite me, Bill, but that's how they treat our boys when they cop 'em, is it! Wish I'd got the devils here who did that, I'd put them through it double quick, that I would!" replied the corporal, white with rage.

The Germans had been effectively cleared from that section of the village, and the men gathered in little groups for a few seconds to get a breather, and to reform one of the sections and companies, ready for another advance if called upon. A dozen of them crowded around the dead scouts, and every one of them, when they saw the handkerchief round John Holland's forehead, and understood what it meant, vowed vengeance upon the first German who should fall into their hands.

"They ain't human beings, an' they ain't fit to live alongside human beings," said one man.

" An' they ain't agoin' to live alongside 'em ef I can cop 'em," said his right hand man.

"Left incline there, lads! Let the cavalry get past. Some of Byng's mounted men coming by to clear the woods, I expect," cried a sergeant as the sharp clatter of hoofs was heard coming towards them round a bend near by.

"Look out, lads," shouted another voice. "They're not our men, they're Uhlans, trying to get back to their own lines."

"Uhlans—Uhlans! Stop 'em!" came from a dozen throats.

The Prussians were about twenty strong. It was Lieutenant von Hessler, John Holland's murderer, and his party who had gone forward under cover of the woods to reconnoitre and had now been compelled to return and seek safety. They found themselves in a trap, but hoped to ride through the scattered groups of Worcesters and Highlanders. They might just as well have tried to ride through the North Sea, for the Worcesters were not in a mood just then to let a single German ride anywhere.

"C Company, line the road, smartly." It was done.

"Present — fire!" cried the sergeant in charge for the moment.

At the first volley half the horsemen fell to the ground. At the second volley there was not a mounted man left. A few minutes of hand-to-hand fighting with those who had dismounted finished the ugly business. Lieutenant von Hessler himself, his horse having been shot under him at the first volley, leapt to the ground, and placed his back against the identical tree where, less than an hour before, he had ordered the scout-master to be shot as a spy.

There he fought with a revolver in both hands, killing a Highlander and wounding several other men. In fact, it seemed as if he might make good his escape after all, but some one shouted just then :—

"Remember Maxwell's Eagles !"

It was the corporal of the Worcesters, who, seeing the others busily engaged, dashed in upon his assailant, and with his clubbed musket, brained him where he stood.

The revolvers fell from the man's hands, and he dropped lifeless to the ground. Thus was justice, rude and swift, meted out to this man, though never one of his opponents knew that he had been the grim avenger of John Holland.

When the village had been made secure against another counter-attack from the Germans, the bodies of the dead were removed for burial, and amongst them the remains of the three Eagles were tenderly carried away, and buried together in a little orchard near by, for, in searching for the dead, they came across the body of Shackleton. And a little wooden cross marks the spot where they were buried, and on it the corporal of the Worcesters carved these letters :—

"HERE LIE BURIED THREE OF MAXWELL'S EAGLES WHO DIED FOR ENGLAND."

When this came to the ears of the General of the Division, he was greatly distressed, and asked that search should be made for the rest of the patrol, fearing that they also had met a similar fate, but they were nowhere to be found. Unless, therefore, they had been buried amid some of the ruins, they must have been taken prisoners. For several days inquiries were made for them amongst the various Brigades,

until at length they were given up for lost, and
the men of that Division when they spoke of
Maxwell's Eagles, as they often did with great
tenderness, for they were greatly beloved, always spoke of them as "the lost patrol."

And in the next dispatch which was sent
from Flanders to England they were mentioned as—

"The Lost Patrol who have Rendered
Undying Service to the Cause of
England."

Thus did the Eagle Patrol win its laurels on
the battle-field and become enshrined in the
hearts of the people of these Islands.

They are not lost, however, who live and
die for England, and though for a while their
sun had set and dark days of exile and imprisonment were before them, yet the day was
coming when their sun would rise again, and
the undimmed lustre of their glory be greater
than ever.

So for a while in England the daily papers
were full of the deeds of heroism performed
by the lads of the Eagle Patrol.   And though
into a few homes there crept a dark shadow at

the news of their loss, yet in more than one
village and township many a young heart was
stirred to emulate the courage and manly
daring of these brave lads who had gone forth
in jeopardy of their lives.

Like a trumpet call to the youth of England
came the story of Maxwell's Eagles. And
from the farm and the smithy, the workshop
and the mine, they came forth, leaving the
plough and the anvil behind, to march in the
ranks of freedom, for they were Freedom's
sons, and they disdained the tyrant's yoke.

CHAPTER XX.

PRISONERS OF WAR.

AFTER two days of travelling, sometimes on foot and partly by train from Aix-la-Chapelle, the four Eagles reached Deuz, the German fortress on the Rhine opposite Cologne. From thence they were removed on the third day, after having been examined by several Prussian officers, to a place further up the river, called Rolandseck, where the Rhine cuts its way through the ragged, mountainous country called the Drachenfels, or Sieben-Berge.

In this lonely but picturesque place they were interned for three weeks, in a small camp of tents, wooden huts, and brick buildings, while every day they were compelled to work for their captors. Sometimes they were taken to the Island of Grafenwerth, in the middle of the river, or to Rhondorf, a village near by, but always they were guarded by Landsturm men with loaded rifles and fixed bayonets, and were repeatedly given to understand that on the first attempt to escape they would be instantly shot. With them were interned several Belgians, Russians and Frenchmen.

Fortunately, the four Eagles were permitted to remain together, and to occupy the same room at night, which was on the ground floor, just near the end of the sentry's walk.

December came, and the peaks of the Drachenfels on the other side of the river were already capped with snow, but so far, although the Eagles had repeatedly talked over their chances of escape, not a single chance had offered. The whole position was full of difficulty, for there were only two pathways down that steep mountain side, and these were both well guarded, while the broad, swift waters of the Rhine half-circled the base of the hill where they were interned.

"What do you think about it all, Danby?" Bancroft whispered to the patrol-leader one cold night, when, after their basin of potato soup, they huddled closer together for warmth, and began to talk for the twentieth time of their chances of escape.

"Where is the sentry, Bancroft?"

"Listen!—he's right at the other end. I can hear him stamping his feet to keep warm. You may talk freely for a minute."

"Well, I've been thinking it over all day, and I have come to the conclusion that we cannot delay it much longer. The food's terrible and it gets more scanty every day. Half the fellows are down with the fever too. It's the bad food more than anything else; they want us to die. Well now——"

"Hist! here comes the sentry again."

And for the next few seconds they were all quiet, pretending to sleep, while the sentry flashed an electric torch in their direction. They pretended to be alarmed and called out, asking what was the matter.

"Gut—sehr gut!" mumbled the German in a guttural voice, and, stamping his feet again, started once more on his little circuit.

As soon as he had gone, Danby pulled from under his now ragged coat a broken piece of hard steel.

"See that?" he whispered.

"What is it?" they asked.

"A broken pick. One of the Belgians broke his tool to-day, and a little piece of it fell near to me. I immediately seized it and hid it under my clothes."

" Good. But what can we do with it ? " asked Willoughby.

" Loosen a few bricks under the bed there and make a man-hole."

" Ripping ! " they all agreed, their despondency vanishing like a cloud, now that a slight chance offered itself for escape.

Now, the four beds were arranged in two tiers on the side of an inner wall, which was evidently not very thick, for they had frequently heard sounds coming through the partition. So it was arranged that each night one of them should be continually at work loosening the bricks, in an arranged area, under the bottom bunk ; the bricks to remain in position till they were all removed together, when the opportunity served.

Danby took the first shift that night, and, lying full length under the bottom bunk, chipped and scratched away until the sentry returned again, which was every five minutes. When Danby had worked for half an hour, Bancroft took his turn, and so on. Every time the sentry approached the work was stopped suddenly, while the scouts chatted freely as though nothing was happening.

This went on for six or seven nights, until at length there came one afternoon when the barometer fell rapidly, and a blinding snow-storm came on, wrapping the mountains, the river, and the land in a curtain of white flakes, through which it was impossible to see more than twenty yards.

The Eagles were out at Rhondorf that afternoon, working in the fields with some of the other prisoners. The guards became alarmed, and shot a couple of the Belgians who attempted to escape.

"Prisoners—fall in!" ordered the Landsturm sergeant under whose charge they had been working.

When this was done, they were numbered and marched rapidly to the river-bank and taken across in boats to Rolandseck.

"Keep close together, lads," Danby had whispered. "We shall not have long to wait now."

They trusted Danby implicitly, and followed every minute instruction he was able to pass on to them.

"Don't try to get away now," he added, as they passed the Island of Nonnenwerth in mid-stream. "The storm will get worse this evening, and the guard will be sure to be relaxed, as I see several men have got away, and they will start in pursuit as soon as they have taken us back and locked us up safely. Then will be our chance. Don't do anything to arouse their suspicions."

They were soon landed and taken to the little building near the castle ruins, where they had been previously kept. Supper was served out to them earlier, and, as Danby had anticipated, some of the guards started off in pursuit of those who had already attempted an escape.

"Crash! Crash!" came the thunder, and the lightning flashed from peak to peak amongst the crags of the Drachenfels.

"What a night!" exclaimed Willoughby, as the building shook again and again with the force of the wind which howled and raged without.

"Just the night we want, Eagles!" replied Danby. "We shall be free before morning if this continues. Are you all ready?"

15

"Yes, ready!" they replied.

"Just listen for the sentry, Bancroft, while I remove the bricks."

"Aye, aye, sir!"

Then Danby went to work, and in three minutes he had removed the nine bricks, to loosen which they had worked for seven nights. He was about to creep back from under the bunk, when Bancroft whistled the first bar of the hymn

Oft in danger, oft in woe,

which had been for them a danger-signal long before they left England. Evidently he had seen or heard the sentry, who had been taking longer rounds that night. Danby stopped still, but the other boys chatted away, and began arguing in a loud voice to cover the delinquent.

"Thump—thump!" came a couple of bangs at the door. It was the sentry, and he was peering through the little grill.

They crowded round the narrow opening, and asked him a few questions, but he was a new man, and spoke no English. He seemed a bit dull and stupid, and smelt of drink, as though the discipline had been relaxed somewhat. In a moment he had gone.

"All clear?" asked Danby in a low voice.

"Yes, all clear," replied Bancroft.

"Come along, then, quietly, and bring those crusts of bread; we shall need them, even if they are a bit mouldy."

The patrol-leader went through the hole first, Willoughby and Murphy followed, and Bancroft came last. Once through the hole in the wall, they found themselves in another room, with windows looking down on to the river, and standing there for a few seconds, Danby could distinctly see the water every time a flash of lightning lit up the sky.

"Look around there, smartly!" whispered their leader. "This is a guard-room, and they have all gone to recover the fellows who bolted when we were in the fields. Pick up a few things."

In less than a minute each lad had secured either a blanket or a coat and hat; one got a bayonet, another a heavy stick, while Danby actually found a loaded revolver, which some one had unintentionally left there. A loaf of bread was also secured, and then the patrol-leader whispered :—

"Now follow me as soon as the next flash has gone by."

The flash came and went, and Danby, seeing the coast clear and no one in sight, unslid the window-catch and dropped out, some six or seven feet to the ground. The rest followed in a twinkling.

At last they were free, but what next?

"This way, Eagles," called their leader, for he had thought out every detail of the plan of escape. The darkness favoured them, and they followed close at his heels, crouching down for a little while. This led them over some rough sloping ground towards the little winding path that led to the river.

The tempest was at its height; it was now a veritable blizzard. If the scouts had separated, even for a moment, they would have lost each other. The flashes of lightning were their chief danger, however, for sometimes the sky was alight for twenty seconds together with successive flashes.

They had found the path now, and were slowly creeping down the hill, holding each other's hands, when Danby, catching sight of something ahead like a glint of steel during another flash, whispered :—

" Eagles, take cover ! "

It was done smartly, for the ground was rocky and broken on either hand. Another flash came, and revealed to them the sentry, returning from the lower camp; he was but twenty paces away. They could hear his footsteps now ; he was close upon them, and their hearts beat wildly. Suddenly, the man stopped and cried :—

" Himmel ! Was ist das ? "

Something had happened ! What could it be ? Were they discovered ?

The scouts remained with their faces pressed to the earth, hidden behind the rocks and boulders. They scarcely dared to breathe. This was their first attempt at escape, and it threatened to end in disaster.

Poor Willoughby, the smallest of the lads, felt his heart thumping loudly ; so loudly, in fact, that he feared that it would betray his presence.

The sentry, however, seemed to be speaking to himself, muttering something, gibbering and chattering as if with fright.   He was not the usual sentry, but evidently a rustic recruit.

"Gott!   Mein Gott!" he was heard to exclaim several times ; the rest was inaudible.

CHAPTER XXI.

THE DRACHENFELS.

DANBY was the least perturbed of all, and from behind his shelter he covered the dark blur of the sentry with the revolver. The shot would never be heard in that gale. The real danger was that another flash of lightning might reveal the Eagles to the man, and thus show the path they were taking, which was towards the river. In that case, there was nothing else for it. The safety of the lads under his charge would be endangered and the trigger would be pulled.

For half a minute the man halted, and stood staring in the direction of the castle ruins, at the very summit of the hill.

" Flash—flicker—flash ! " came the lightning again, and a terrific peal of thunder seemed to split the mountain, shaking it so that stones were loosened and began to roll down the hill-side. In that moment Danby saw the man's face clear and distinct, and could scarcely restrain himself from laughter. He pocketed his shooting-iron, for there was no immediate need for it, from that quarter at least.

The fact was, the sentry was terrified by fear of the ghosts up in the ruined Castle of Rolandseck, where for nine hundred years weird and fearful legends of ghostly visitants have terrified the simple inhabitants of the villages and hamlets about the Drachenfels. Strange stories were current of Knight Roland and the fair Hildegunde, who dwelt at the little convent down below, on the Island of Nonnenwerth.

"Wie geistlick!" exclaimed the terrified sentry, crossing himself, for until war had broken out he had been but a simple rustic, and his brain had been half-turned latterly by the weird and ghostly tales he had heard about the supernatural visitants of Roland-seck.

In another minute the danger was passed, for the sentry had moved on, and Danby, collecting his little band, proceeded warily down the steep, zigzag pathway.

"Quick! This way, Eagles!" he exclaimed, when at length they reached the river-bank. "The boat should be somewhere here. Keep your eyes well-skinned for it when the next flash comes," for their leader had taken mental notes of everything likely to assist their escape.

"Phew!—here it comes," cried some one, as another blue flash lit up the river, and laid bare not only the surface of the water but the peaks of the Sieben-Berge and the ruins of another castle opposite.

"The boat—there she is, sir!" exclaimed Willoughby, who had caught a glimpse of her, not fifty feet away, at the very spot where they had left her but three hours before.

"Capital! Lead the way, Willoughby, and see if you can find her in the dark," ordered Danby.

A moment later they had found her, baled her out—for she was inches deep in snow and water—and had tumbled aboard.

"Take the oars, Bancroft and Murphy, and pull for all you are worth when I give you the tip. And, I say, Willoughby, get into her bow, and keep a sharp look-out for a good landing-place on the other side, or we may strike a rock and go to pieces with this howling gale and the rapid current, for it's racing past us like a mill-pond."

"Rhenus flumen rapidum est," remarked Bancroft coolly, as he feathered his oar for an instant, waiting for the word of command.

"All ready?" cried Danby.

"Aye, aye, sir!"

"Then go!"

And with that, the patrol-leader cut the painter which held the boat fast to the shore, and they were whirled away into the rushing stream.

"Pull for all you're worth, while I keep her nose up!" came from the stern, and they tugged at the oars like Trojans.

Despite their efforts, however, they were carried much further down stream than they desired to go, for the current was fearful. In addition, owing to the violence of the wind, the boat rocked and tossed about like a cork. It was almost madness to tempt the waters of the Rhine on a night like this, in the darkness too. Fortunately, they were just below the two Islands of Grafenwerth and Nonnenwerth, else they would have been hurled ashore there by the rapid downward drift. For half an hour they battled with the elements, and almost gave it up in despair, when a friendly flash revealed to them the other bank, not twenty yards away.

"Smart there, Willoughby!"

"Yes, sir. Another three good strokes and we shall do it. We're in shallow water with soft mud," cried the youth in the bows. Then immediately after he ordered, "Ship oars! She's aground!"

"Thank heaven! We couldn't have lasted another five minutes. We should have been swamped, but now we're safe!" exclaimed Danby, leaping from the water-logged boat into the shallow water. Then clambering up the bank, he turned and gave the others a hand up.

"Where are we?" they exclaimed, sitting down for an instant to recover breath, especially Bancroft and Murphy, who were just about dead-beat.

"We're almost at the bottom of the Drachenfels. A road runs somewhere here along the margin of the river. When you've had a breather, we'll find it, and get along. If we can get amongst the Sieben-Berge, we can hide there for weeks if necessary until the hunt cools off. It's all mountains, crags and forests, with caves and precipices. A tender-foot could hide there for months."

"Any grub there?" asked Willoughby, sucking one of the mouldy crusts he had brought with him.

"Oh, we'll manage the grub somehow, if we've got to lay snares and poach by day, and come down to the river to net fish at nights. The Eagles are not the sort of fellows to starve if there's any game about, eh, what say you, Banky, old fellow?"

"You may safely trust the Eagle Patrol for that, sir!" replied Bancroft, whose natural aptitude for laying a snare had nearly landed him into trouble when at school.

"Now, boys, we'd better be starting. They may miss us any moment at the camp. Follow me. Phew! How it blows still. Never mind, it's all in our favour, but we must find a snug hole somewhere before daybreak," said Danby, starting off, followed by the others.

"Hullo! What's this?" he whispered almost immediately afterwards.

" Barbed wire ? " suggested Murphy, bringing out a pair of clippers he had boned from the guard-room.

" Feels like it too," said another.   " It's gone through my clothes and made a bad rip."

" H'm ! we're up against the Rhine defences, then.   Hope there are no more sentries about. Crawl under, boys, and don't use the clippers, Murphy, or we shall show the pack where to follow us to-morrow."

" The boat will show that, sir," replied the bugler, pocketing the snippers.

" No, it won't.   I shoved it off and it's a mile down stream by this time, probably up against the bridge of boats at Bonn or Cologne."

So they crawled under the entanglements, which were evidently preparatory defences against an enemy-crossing, later in the campaign, but no sentry appeared to challenge them.   Then they clambered up the steep slope of the hill, passing near the Drachenhöhle, or Dragon's cave, in which lived the old monster slain by Siegfried long, long ago. Then up and on they went in the darkness for another three hours, stumbling, lurching, falling over rough, broken ground, and on until they reached the Sieben-Berge proper, and here at length they found a cave in the hill-side, where they rested.

They were now utterly exhausted, so they ate the loaf of dark rye bread which they had brought, and then rolled themselves in the wet blankets which they had dragged with them, and slept soundly for three hours.

It was nearly dawn when Danby awoke. He could have slept for hours longer; for days he thought. But he had forced himself to wake by sheer will-power, for he had many things to think about, and the safety and welfare of the remnant of the patrol depended upon his leadership.

He knew not where the dawn would find them. They might be under the very eyes of German pickets, or near some habitation, whose dwellers might give them away. Carefully, therefore, he crept towards the mouth of the cave and looked around, just as the first faint tinge of light lit up the eastern sky.

"Good!" he ejaculated. "Not a human soul is in sight; nor a single habitation."

The land was rough and mountainous,

though spotted with herbage, woods, and with broken streams in the gullies.

"Hist! What was that, though?" he asked himself, as a slight movement startled him. He peeped cautiously around in the dim light, and then fixed his eyes in the direction from whence the sound came.

Something was moving just a few yards away; a dim object lower down the slope. Then he heard a crisp, grinding noise. His hand instinctively crept to his revolver, and he pointed it, but did not fire, afraid lest the report should bring unwelcome guests.

"What was it? Yes, surely it was an animal; some four-footed creature. Ha! a mountain-goat. Good!"

He smacked his lips, for he was hungry, and there was food—good food, such as he had not tasted for many, many weeks. At all costs it must be secured quietly, killed and cooked. It would serve them for food for a fortnight.

Suddenly, a hand was laid upon his shoulder. He started and turned his head, but it was only Bancroft, who had heard him wake up, and had crawled out to see what was the matter.

"Oh, Leslie," he whispered, "there is our

breakfast, if only you could have brought your lasso."

"So I did," replied Bancroft. "I picked up a coil of rope as we left the guard-room. It's not my own though, but I can manage a simple throw like this with it." Having said which he crept back and half a minute later appeared again with the rope.

"One—two—three! Gee whiz! I've got him!" and before the terrified animal could utter so much as a sound, the rope was drawn tight around its neck, and the two lads, leaping down the slope, captured and dragged it into the cave half-strangled.

What followed can easily be imagined. The goat was quickly killed, skinned and hung up. A fire of dry sticks, collected chiefly from within the cave, was lit. These would show very little smoke. Soon, four or five pounds of goat's flesh was being grilled.

"Golly, but that smells heavenly!" cried Murphy, who had slept till that moment. "Where on earth did you get——"

"Wake up there, smartly, Willoughby and Murphy," cried Danby, cutting him short. "Are you going to sleep the whole day?"

"I was just dreaming that breakfast was ready at home, sir, in dear Old England, when I woke up, and found this heavenly aroma filling the cave," exclaimed Willoughby, sitting up and rubbing his eyes, as the result of a smart punch from Murphy.

"Get out of the cave, both of you, smartly now and scout round. If anybody sees this smoke, or smells this aroma, we've got to quit. Understand?"

"Yes, sir."

"Be smart, then, and if all goes well you shall have the breakfast of your life in half an hour."

"Oh, scrumptious! Oh, beautiful! I am that hungry, I could eat the blamed thing raw. How-be-so-ever, here goes! Half an hour, you said, Danby?"

"Yes, half an hour. Out you go!"

"Say twenty minutes, there's a good fellow, and I'll be your fag for the rest of my life."

"I said half an hour," returned the patrol-leader peremptorily.

"Right, sir!" answered Willoughby, remaining for another half-minute to sniff the savoury atmosphere about the camp-fire.

16

"How do you expect that I can cook a three course dinner in twenty minutes, you young cub?"

"Eh, what's that you say, sir? A three course dinner?"

"Yes, here's the menu, look :—

"Chèvre de montagne :—

First	course	. .	roasted.
Second	„	. .	boiled.
Third	„ .	. .	grilled."

"Oh, glorious! Oh, scrumptious!" exclaimed the lad, and with that he followed Murphy, and they scouted round, keeping well under cover, with their eyes and ears open towards the world outside and around, but with all their olfactory nerves strained in the direction of that coming meal.

CHAPTER XXII.

THE RETURN OF THE EAGLES.

THAT morning the Eagles breakfasted right royally on savoury goat's flesh and bread crusts. It was the most satisfying meal they had had for many months, and they washed it down with a deep draught of cold water which ran down the nearest gully.

Then, having cleared away all traces of the camp-fire, lest it should betray them, they re-entered the cave, and decided to remain hidden during the day, as they knew that a careful search would be made for them.

It was well that they did so, for that day, from their hiding-place, where they were carefully screened, they observed no fewer than five separate parties of German soldiers and police, who were doubtless hunting for them with fire-arms. It was almost by a miracle that they were saved. At any rate, the boys

all decided that a kindly Providence had inter-
fered on their behalf.

That morning, when they re-entered the
cave, Murphy raised his stick to knock down
a huge spider that was patching up the broken
web which they had disturbed at their first
entry, but Danby checked him just in time, by
seizing his arm, and saying :—

"Don't be a fool, Murphy! That spider
may save our lives to-day. Remember Robert
Bruce and let the spider live."

Some of the boys laughed at this, but subsequent events proved that the patrol-leader
was right. Most of that morning, after having removed every vestige of tell-tale foot-
marks, they sat resting in the dark recess,
watching the industrious spider patiently toil-
ing to mend the gap. Never once did he rest
from his labour till long after noon, when the
rent was neatly finished.

Soon after this they saw the first party of
searchers, looking everywhere, down the
gullies, in the holes of the tree trunks, and
amid the rocks and boulders. A little later
they saw a second and third party, and it was
this latter group that nearly discovered them.

So near were they that they could hear their voices outside the cave, and one man approached so closely that Danby covered him with his revolver.

"Hist!" whispered the leader, raising his finger, as one of the boys in moving rustled a few leaves.

Slight though it was, the sound seemed to have reached the German. He turned round sharply, and espied the narrow cleft which served as the opening of the cave.

"Ach, Himmel!" they heard him exclaim, and immediately they heard him call a second man.

"Nein, nein!" replied the other in answer to some query. "Es giebt nicht da!"

"Warum nicht?" said the first.

"Sehen Sie nicht die Spinne!" answered the second, pointing to the spider's web, which by this time entirely closed the narrow entrance.

It was sufficient evidence for them both, and deciding not to waste further valuable time, they departed to search further afield.

"Marvellous!" exclaimed Murphy. "You were quite right, Danby. That spider has

probably saved our lives.   I will never kill another spider as long as I live."

"Nor I!   Nor I!"added the others.

"And when we leave this place," cried
Willoughby, "I will take that fine fellow with
me and make a pet of him.   Yes, take him to
'Blighty' I will, for he is too much of a gentleman to live in Germany."   At which the others
laughed, but so he did, and made a little
wooden box for the fellow with his pen-
knife, and carried him for weeks, feeding
him carefully, and teaching him to come at his
call.

So for no less than six weeks the Eagles remained about the country of the Drachenfels,
trapping rabbits, hares, and other wild
creatures ; snaring birds and sometimes, during the night, venturing down to the river-bank
to fish with a few primitive hooks and nets
which they had made for themselves.   And
when they tired of fish, flesh and fowl, they
went further afield and stole a few turnips,
potatoes and artichokes to vary their diet.

They lived like Crusoes, fending for themselves, sometimes changing their place of
abode, for they had plenty of choice in that

wild, desolate land of the Seven Mountains. Their scout-craft had made them so clever and cunning that they had no great wish to change their mode of life for the dangers of the open country, where they might easily have been discovered, until one day their longing for news of the war and the homeland became so intense that they ran a great risk in order to satisfy their longings.   It happened thus :—

One morning they were hiding in their cave as usual, resting after the fatigues of another successful night's sport, and watching Old Tim the spider doing a canter across his web after some fly that had been tempted out by the first gleam of early spring, when they heard voices without.

"Hist, boys!" came the usual caution from Danby, and they lay still scarcely daring to breathe, but wondering hard who it could be that was treading the wild paths of the Drachenfels so early in the spring.   But as the voices came nearer, some one whispered :—

"They're speaking in English too!   Who can they be?"

"More escaped prisoners, perhaps," suggested Bancroft faintly, nudging Danby.

"No, Americans!" whispered the patrol-leader.

" Really ? "

" Yes, no doubt about it ; but listen, they're sure to be talking about the war, and I want to hear what they're saying."

" Yas, I calculate it'll be a long war, an' that America will have to come in to help the British lion at the finish."

" I reckon she ought to have done that afore this, but come in she must for the sake of humanity," replied the second.

That was all they heard as the two men passed, but it was sufficient to show them that they were friends, though what had brought two American tourists to that part of the world so early in the season puzzled them somewhat.   Danby noticed that one of the travellers carried a newspaper under his arm, and when they were out of earshot, he remarked to the others :—

" I would give something to see that news-paper which one of them carried. I shall fol-low their trail, and if he drops it or throws it away I will bring it back. It is sure to be an

English copy, and will give us the news we want so badly."

The others demurred at this, and spoke of the risk to which Danby would be exposing himself in the daytime, as several enemy patrols had been seen about the place lately. The patrol-leader, however, promised that he would use the utmost care, and in no case would he betray their hiding-place. Then he slipped out quietly.

Twenty minutes later he was back again with the coveted newspaper, which had been thrown away by its owner.

"Great news!" he cried.

"What is it?" they all asked eagerly, leaping to their feet and surrounding him.

"There has been a sea-fight off the Falkland Islands. Seven German ships have been sunk, including four large cruisers; only a small cruiser got away, and that is now being chased round Cape Horn by the British sea-dogs."

"Hurrah! hurrah!" they cried, unable to restrain themselves at this welcome news of Admiral Sturdee's victory, which had thus come to them by a belated newspaper. It was a copy of the "Daily Telegraph" which had brought them these tidings across the sea and over hundreds of miles of the enemy's territory. Very quickly they divided the paper up so that each had a portion, every line and letter of which was read.

Suddenly, Willoughby uttered an exclamation of joy and surprise ; then throwing down his sheet of the paper, he began to dance and caper about as though possessed.

"What is the matter?" they asked.

"Matter?" he replied. "Look there!"

They did look as well as the dim light of the cave would permit, and this is what they read from a small paragraph in the middle of the paper :—

"THE LOST PATROL.

"YESTERDAY, A TABLET WAS UNVEILED ON THE SOUTH WALL OF WESTMINSTER ABBEY TO THE MEMORY OF MAXWELL'S EAGLES, THE LOST PATROL, WHO RENDERED UNDYING SERVICE TO ENGLAND. FOR THEIR BRAVE DEEDS THEY WERE MENTIONED IN DISPATCHES, AND ONE OF THEM RECEIVED THE V.C. THEY WERE ALL LOST AT THE BATTLE OF YPRES,"

Then the names of the patrol were given and a special tribute was paid to John Holland. The tablet was unveiled by the Chief Scout in the presence of the Dean and Chapter, and had been subscribed for by their old school-fellows, who were present on the occasion.

The Eagles could scarcely believe their eyes when they read all this. The tears welled up, and they were moved more deeply than they had ever been since the tragic death of John Holland. To think that they had been thus honoured by their country, and remembered by their school-fellows. For the rest of that day they could speak of nothing else. Even Sturdee's victory was almost forgotten.

Their only thought now was to return home. All the romance of their Crusoe life began to fade away. One and all determined that they must get back, whatever the risk they ran.

It would not be possible to tell all their adventures in the Drachenfels, which would fill another book, and we must come to the time when, after many hair-breadth escapes and great hardships, the Eagles managed to smuggle aboard the " Kinderdijk," one of the river steamers belonging to a Dutch company and running between Rotterdam and Maintz. How they escaped the vigilant police and customs, and eventually, aided by a friendly steward and a fireman of Dutch nationality, whose only brother had been shot by the Germans, managed to crawl out of the coal-bunker, when they had passed the last German village of Emmerich, where the Rhine becomes the Maas and enters the territory of Holland—all this must be told another time. Suffice it to say, their good luck did not desert them.

Soon they reached Zalt Bommel and Nymwegen, then shortly afterwards they came to Rotterdam, almost alongside the "Batavier," which was just preparing to sail to the Thames. They quickly secured a passage through the efforts of the British Consul, and before long, sailing down the Maas, they passed the Hook of Holland, and entered the North Sea.

Only one other exciting incident befell them. As they approached the Noord Hinder Lightship, a German patrol-boat drew up, and, after several signals, asked :—

" Have you any English subjects aboard ? "

Here was a dilemma. The captain was

anxious to screen the Eagles, having heard some of their story from the British Consul, and he hesitated for a moment in his reply. The German's suspicions were thereby aroused, and he signalled :—

" Heave to.   Am sending a boat to examine passengers and crew."

" Phew ! " exclaimed Danby, who had read the signals, for they had been flown in the international code.   " It looks like trouble again."

The boat was half-way across when suddenly she was recalled by another signal.   What was the matter ?

" Matter enough ! " cried some one.   " Just look there ! "

They did look ; every passenger crowding to the side.   Away to the west was the smoke of a British destroyer coming up full pelt.   This it was which the German had seen.   It was quite enough.   Though he had recalled the boat, he could not wait for it.   He actually abandoned his own men and fled for the shelter of his mine beds or neutral waters.

" You rascal ! " exclaimed a passenger, shaking his fist at the departing German.   " Why don't you stop to fight ? You don't mind threatening an unarmed ship, but when you see a bit o' thunder you run like the devil."

But even this manœuvre did not save him. The destroyer was a racer and was doing nearly forty knots, with the flames coming out of her funnels. As she raced up past the "Batavier," she opened fire upon the retreating vessel. With the third shot she found her mark, and with her tenth she sent the patrol to the bottom. Then, swirling round, she picked up a few survivors from the water, hauled aboard the boat's crew which had been abandoned, and was back alongside the "Batavier" in less than twenty minutes.

As she came up, she caught a signal from the Dutch boat. It was to tell of the presence of the Eagles. A moment later a smart sub-lieutenant came aboard, and heard the whole story.

"Maxwell's Eagles?" he said. "But they're all dead. My young brother was at the same school, and he told me all about them in his last letter."

"Four of 'em here are very much alive, at any rate," said some one.

Ten minutes later, a wireless message from

the destroyer carried the tidings to England, and an hour later, when the papers in Fleet Street and Ludgate Hill came out with such headlines as—

"MAXWELL'S EAGLES COMING HOME—THE LOST PATROL FOUND," ETC.,

there was great excitement, for the loss of these brave lads had stirred the people of England deeply.

A great welcome was arranged for them, and when the "Batavier" drew in by the Tower Bridge, and berthed by the Customs House in the Pool, there were thousands of people lining the streets and the bridges. Billingsgate was blocked by a great crowd, while from the parapets of London Bridge there came a cry of—

"WELCOME HOME—MAXWELL'S EAGLES."

THE END.